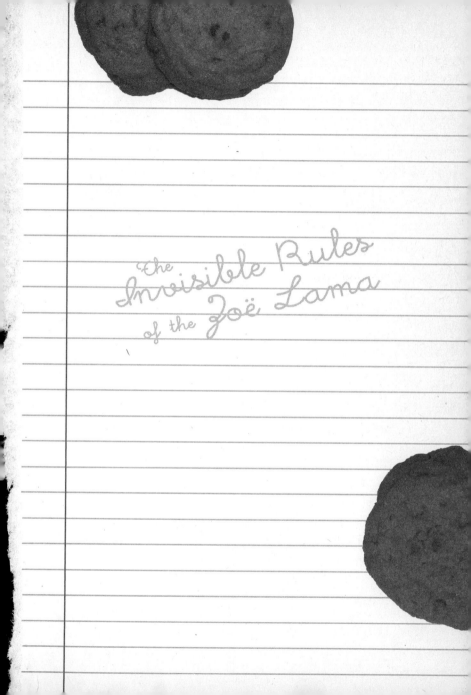

The Invisible Rules of the Zoë Lama

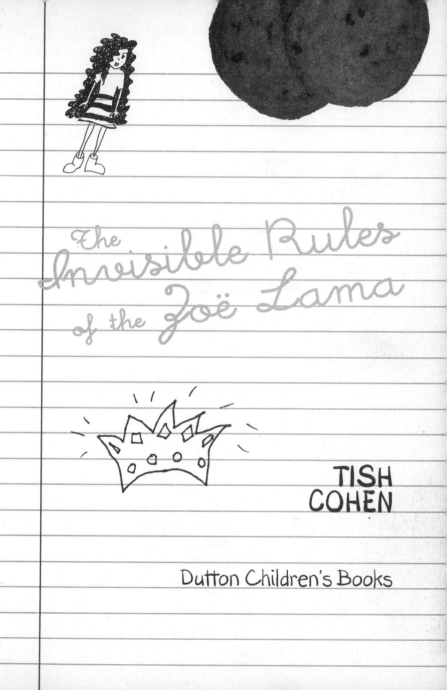

The Invisible Rules of the Zoë Lama

TISH COHEN

Dutton Children's Books

DUTTON CHILDREN'S BOOKS
A division of Penguin Young Readers Group
Published by the Penguin Group
Penguin Group (USA) Inc., 375 Hudson Street, New York, New York 10014, U.S.A.
Penguin Group (Canada), 90 Eglinton Avenue East, Suite 700, Toronto, Ontario, Canada M4P 2Y3
(a division of Pearson Penguin Canada Inc.) • Penguin Books Ltd, 80 Strand, London WC2R 0RL,
England • Penguin Ireland, 25 St Stephen's Green, Dublin 2, Ireland (a division of Penguin Books Ltd)
Penguin Group (Australia), 250 Camberwell Road, Camberwell, Victoria 3124, Australia (a division of
Pearson Australia Group Pty Ltd) • Penguin Books India Pvt Ltd, 11 Community Centre, Panchsheel
Park, New Delhi – 110 017, India • Penguin Group (NZ), 67 Apollo Drive, Rosedale, North Shore
0745, Auckland, New Zealand (a division of Pearson New Zealand Ltd) • Penguin Books (South Africa)
(Pty) Ltd, 24 Sturdee Avenue, Rosebank, Johannesburg 2196, South Africa
Penguin Books Ltd, Registered Offices: 80 Strand, London WC2R 0RL, England

This book is a work of fiction. Names, characters, places, and incidents are either the product of the
author's imagination or are used fictitiously, and any resemblance to actual persons, living or dead,
business establishments, events, or locales is entirely coincidental.

The publisher does not have any control over and does not assume any responsibility for author
or third-party websites or their content.

Library of Congress Cataloging-in-Publication Data
Cohen, Tish, date.
The invisible rules of the Zoë Lama / by Tish Cohen. — 1st ed.
p. cm.
Summary: Twelve-year-old Zoe, famous for advising other people using her unwritten rules, has
her hands full with chairing a school dance committee, training a new student to fit in, keeping her
grandmother out of a nursing home, and trying to find a husband for her mother.
ISBN: 978-0-525-47810-2 (hardcover: alk paper) [1. Interpersonal relations—Fiction. 2. Middle
schools—Fiction. 3. Schools—Fiction. 4. Grandmothers—Fiction. 5. Mothers and daughters—Fiction.
6. Alzheimer's disease—Fiction.] I. Title.
PZ7.C66474Inv 2007
[Fic]—dc22   2006024799

Published in the United States by Dutton Children's Books,
a division of Penguin Young Readers Group
345 Hudson Street, New York, New York 10014
www.penguin.com/youngreaders

Designed by IRENE VANDERVOORT

Printed in USA   First Edition
1 3 5 7 9 10 8 6 4 2

*To Max, Lucas, Marysa,
Lachlan, Zoë, Jacob, and Olivia*

Acknowledgments

*E*normous thanks go out to many people:
Claudia Gabel, for your early interest and enthusiasm.
My darling editor, Stephanie Owens Lurie, at Dutton
Children's Books, your expertise and your passion for this
book are staggering. Thank you. Sarah Shumway, Associate
Editor at Dutton Children's Books, for your behind-
the-scenes efforts. Iris Tupholme and Lynne Missen at
HarperCollinsCanada, for support and guidance on the
snowier side of the border.
The witty and talented Daniel Lazar, my literary agent at
Writers House and #1 BFIB. Your wisdom and insight never
fail to astonish me. Nice little idea you had, no? Maja Nikolic
of Writers House, for working hard to get Zoë a passport.
Steve, for laughing first.
And, finally, my Official Middle-Grade Consultants, Max
and Lucas, who hurried home from school every day to
find out what on earth Zoë might muddle up next.

Contents

The
Invisible Rules
of the Zoë Lama

Name Names

I don't like Mondays.

It has nothing at all to do with the weekend being over before you really started having any sort of fun. And that you're now stuck at school behind a desk with not one, not two, not even three, but *four* monster wads of gum stuck underneath it and one metal leg that is miles too short, so the desk wobbles every time you print your name, and the teacher squints and holds her finger to her lips.

That's not why.

It also, in case you're wondering, has nothing to do with hating to get up at 7:30 in the morning—especially after a weekend of sleeping until *The Garage Girls* comes on TV at nine. Okay, it has a little to do with that. But even if they canceled *The Garage Girls*—which they wouldn't, since every girl at Allencroft Middle School watches it every Saturday—even then I would not like Mondays.

When I'm a big yawner of an adult—although, really, I don't know how "big" I'll ever be since I'm the smallest person I know—I'm going to get a job where Monday is a part of the weekend. Then I could only go to work Tuesday, Wednesday, Thursday, and Friday. It would have to be a short week because of *The Garage Girls*. And the place I work had better sell chocolate chip cookies, because I live on chocolate chips and my grandma once said you should have a job you love. **And that's what I love. Chocolate chips.**

The worst part of Mondays is that my mother goes to work crazy early. So I have to stand on a stool at the kitchen counter and line up Grandma's seven hundred tiny colored pills and sort them into a plastic container divided by the days of the week. Mom always puts too many blue pills into Thursday or not enough pink ones into Tuesday because, she says, "I'm way stressed from the juggling act that is my life."

Don't ask about my father. That would be rude, since I can hardly even remember when he was alive, and if *anyone* deserves to know *anything* at all about him, it's me. He died when I was four and the one and only memory I have of him has to last me the rest of my life.

So, anyway, that's the problem with Mondays.

I'm way STRESSED!

○ ○ ○

*T*his Monday happens to be Picture Day, which means I have more to do than usual. Not only do I have to sort out Grandma and worry that Mom will lose her keys again and be late for work and get fired so we'll have to live under a broken bus until I'm old enough to go out and support the three of us . . . but I have to get a class of twenty-six twelve-year-olds ready for the school photographer. **Last year,** when **I let them fend for themselves,** Pamela Peterman wound up wearing the same blouse as Corinna Lynn Binns, and Tall Paul and Small Paul forgot to change out of their gym shorts.

I didn't care so much about Tall Paul—he's last row, center, so no one can see his bony legs. But, since I'm not only shorter than any other human being in the seventh grade, I'm shorter than all of the sixth grade and exactly 76.6 percent of the *fifth* grade—because of that, Small Paul is always crammed next to me. And last year his scabbed-up knees took all the attention away from my sparkly hairband.

I can't risk it happening again.

I sling my backpack over my homeroom chair and pour a handful of plastic barrettes and colored rubber bands onto my desktop. The other kids will be here any second, and I'd like to be ready.

This much I'm sure of:

–Alice Marriott's mother will botch up her French braids and make her wear the vest with the prancing kittens. If I don't help Alice, her future husband will see this vest in a photo one day, and might think twice about reproducing with her. (And would you blame him? Seriously ... prancing kittens.)

–Martin Granitstein will have maple-syrup stains all over his shirt, so I'll have to give him someone's smelly gym shirt from the bottom of their locker. Thankfully, I packed antibacterial wipes so I can disinfect later.

–Avery Buckner will have smeary glasses. Smeared with who-knows-what. I guess I should be happy he's still too young to have dandruff, because when he's older those glasses'll be covered in white flakes. You can just tell. Again, the wipes will save me.

—And, for sure, for sure, for sure, **Sylvia Smye** will have too many cowlicks in her hair. Cowlicks are nearly as cruel an act of nature as making innocent people so small that strangers stop to talk baby talk at them, causing a certain short person to yell back, **"I'm Twelve Years Old and I Don't Want Your Crappy Candy!"**

Okay, not all true. If Mom says it's okay, I take the candy.

The bell rings and kids start pouring into the classroom. A line forms in the aisle in front of my desk and one by one they move toward me, stopping to twirl just like I showed them on Friday afternoon. Approach, stop, spin, and await your instructions. I take a baggie full of chocolate chips from my desk and gather a few for my first client, my number two BFIS.

Number Two Best Friend in School. Laurel Sterling.

"Happy Monday, O Zoë Lama," she says, making a big embarrassing bow.

I make an I-hate-Monday face, mixed with my don't-call-me-Zoë-Lama face. This basically involves mad eye-brows, scrunched-up eyes, and one side of my lip in a sneer. It's not pretty.

I actually don't hate the Zoë Lama part as much as I pretend to hate it, even though **I didn't exactly sign up to be the ruler of nearly everyone around me.**

It started when I was just a kid. At home, it might have had something to do with not having a father around to do helpful fatherish things, like knowing when to up the bran in Grandma's cereal or how to use clear nail polish to stop a run in Mom's stockings.

With teachers, it just sort of happened. Wa-ay back in kindergarten.

Kindergartners, as everyone knows, are a mess. They've got runny noses, missing teeth, shoes on the wrong feet, and stubby bangs they've sawed off with safety scissors—just to see if it would work. Every time they pull off a boot they lose a sock, and if anyone, anywhere, is going to lick an icy handrail, you can bet your favorite underwear it'll be a kindergartner. Not only that, but they talk with a lisp and fall in love with their teacher.

Well . . . some do.

It's not that I thought Mr. Silverberg was going to leave

Hammens. Meanest kid in the school and, to me, about the size of a giant.

Patrick had cornered little pigeon-toed Leo Loomis at the top of the slide. Patrick had been stealing Leo's popcorn-fund-raiser money all week and was giving him misery for having empty pockets—even though Leo's pockets were only empty because Patrick had emptied them! Still, they weren't any emptier than Patrick's brain.

A crowd of us had gathered at the bottom of the slide, hoping to catch Leo if Patrick got pushy. **That was when Patrick said it.** He asked Leo if Mommy tied his shoelaces together as a baby to teach him to walk like a duck.

I was up that slide in half a second.

"What do you want, Flea?" Patrick said to me, one hand still holding the front of Leo's sweater. "You wanna lose your popcorn money, or just your life?"

I ignored this and sat down. "I was just going to say . . . oh, never mind."

Patrick squinted at me through his evil slits for eyes. "What?"

"Nothing. I can see you're busy."

his wife to marry me. I wasn't stupid. Besides, I barely came up to his knees. I just liked being around him and invented all sorts of reasons to help him. I organized the washable marker bins, shined up the building blocks, and sorted my classmates' boots from biggest to smallest to teacher's.

After a while he started to count on me to help and asked me to pass out papers, help on field trips, and, most importantly, watch the class while he popped out for a smoke—his one and only putrid habit. And when Ms. Narck, the elementary school principal, dropped by, I always had the perfect cover for him—he ran out of burnt-sienna crayons, he accidentally stapled his tie to his thumb, his wife drove her car into a pond.

A six-year-old can dream, can't she?

I learned two things that year. First, even if your teacher's wife's Volvo lands in a pond, eventually she'll probably dry off and go home. Second, if you know your way around a teacher's ego, this whole school thing becomes a breeze.

How I became Zoë Lama to the students something of a legend. It all started at the top jungle gym when **I was still about the Thumbelina,** and it involved Patrick "Th

"Spill it or empty your pockets," he growled.

Dropping a pebble down the yellow slide and watching how fast it tumbled, I said, "It's just that **I guess you haven't heard about the studies.** What researchers are saying about kids who push around other kids. What it says, loud and clear, about their pasts." I leaned down to swipe some sand off my shoe.

By this time Patrick had let go of Leo, who was already sliding headfirst toward safety. Patrick squatted down across from me and sneered. "What do *they* know?"

"Just that bully types come from families where they never feel heard. From parents who spend their every waking moment launching their new vitamin company and hire English nannies to pretend to love their kids." Okay, so my mother gossips about the neighbors. A lot.

It worked like magic. Patrick hid his face from me.

"Some of these parents even forget the little things that make a childhood special. Like the tooth fairy during the agonizing molar years . . ."

He sniffled.

"Or that the bike a certain little boy wished for on his seventh birthday was a shiny red mountain bike with a water-bottle holder, not a crummy blue one with a banana seat and streamers . . ."

He wiped his face with his dirty sleeve.

"That this boy never cared about all those train rides to visit Grandma's penthouse in New York with a spectacular view of the park, all he really wanted was to play Little Red Riding Hood with his dad in the basement."

The crowd below was silent, waiting for Patrick's response. That was when the Raptor, previously known for crushing pop cans against his forehead and stuffing fourth graders through the basketball hoop, began to bawl.

Not wanting to destroy the stupid oaf, I put an arm around his hulking shoulders and gave them a squeeze. **"It's okay, Patrick. Let it all out."**

"Grammie was never even home," he sobbed. "I had to play Scrabble with her veiny old 'gentleman friend'!"

"That's right. Have a good cry. It's how we heal." Okay . . . so my mother had a few self-help books lying around. It wasn't original, but it worked.

He looked up, his cheeks soaked with tears, and sniffed. "You think I can? Heal?"

"Absolutely. You know what you need?"

He shook his head.

"You need a safe place to fall. Someone to share your feelings with. Someone like me."

Kids started whispering and pointing like mad, and from that moment on, they looked at me differently. **I had defused the Raptor and become a schoolyard celebrity** all at once.

And I liked it.

"Wow," said Miss Noonan, the playground monitor, from behind the seesaw. She wormed her way through the crowd of gawking kids and squinted up at me, still at the top of the slide. "You're like a pint-size Dalai Lama. Bringing freedom and the right to coexist in peace and harmony to the peoples of Allencroft Elementary School." She shivered and pulled her cardigan sweater tighter around herself. "You're the Zoë Lama."

Of course, I had to race straight into the library to look up the word *lama*. First I spelled it with two *l*'s and thought Miss Noonan was calling me a "woolly beast of burden." Naturally, I was a little upset. But then the librarian told me *lama*, in some other language, means teacher.

It made perfect sense, since these kids really do need guidance.

And so it was. The Zoë Lama was born.

From that day on, requests came in almost daily for advice ranging from how to break in a new pair of flip-flops with minimal bleeding, to how to crush on a boy in a younger grade without destroying your reputation.

I soon discovered an added bonus. **Being the knower-of-all-unwritten-rules automatically provides me with an *untouchable* reputation**—a happy side effect I'm thankful for every single day. As long as the Zoë Lama reigns, my status is safe. The day my reign ends is the day my peoples will drop the peace-and-harmony crap and eat me alive.

*L*aurel's skirt is pink corduroy. Her sweater is orange to match her tights, and her shoes are greenish with red laces. If it was anyone but Laurel wearing this rainbow of gross-osity, I'd have told them to fake sick and go home. Fast. But Laurel is working hard to change, and when someone works hard at something, they need a reward, don't you think?

Laurel is obsessed with the color blue.

Ever since I've known her, since we napped beside each other at Little Monsters Daycare, she's worn head-to-toe blue. Always. Sometimes she even has to wear boys' stuff, because the girls' sections are mostly pink and red. Not only that, Laurel only *eats* blue stuff. The teachers at Little Monsters used to complain that they didn't have blue snacks for Laurel, except in blueberry season. So Laurel's mother brought snacks from home—blue, of course—in a special container. Blue.

So you can see why I just offer Laurel some chocolate chips (which she refuses, but I have to offer) and nod. Laurel punches me in the shoulder—our secret sign—and sits down behind me, whispering, "Your hair looks good today, not too frizzy and extra chocolaty." **Every morning Laurel gives me the hair report,** whether I want it or not. And since I happen to have especially curly, especially brown hair that happens to be long enough for me to sit on, and it happens to be right there in front of Laurel's face all day long, she also tends to style it. **Whether I like it or not.**

"Thanks," I say. "You can braid it into ten braids, if you want. I'd like to look like a Caribbean princess today." I pass back a few rubber bands to help get her motivated. "But not until after pictures, so I'm not a Caribbean princess forever in my mom's wallet."

Next.

Brianna Simpson is wearing white . . . when I told her specifically that it makes her look sick with her freckles. Now I'll have to slap her cheeks before the camera clicks to make them look pink. Not too hard. Well, kinda hard. But she'll appreciate it when she takes home proofs that make her look like she's just gotten off her steaming pony in the hills of Ireland. Not that she has a steaming pony. Too much dander.

Next is my **number one BFIS. Susannah Barnes.** She looks great, as usual. **She's wearing big dark sunglasses** and stops to lower them so I can see her eyes and know it's her.

Susannah is the perfect best friend. She's a snarky, mocking, complicated drama diva. And don't ever play with her hair or ask to try on her shades, because both are off-limits. But she'll give you her last M&M, she'll remember exactly what you wanted for your birthday, and she'll phone you at 6 A.M. to remind you to wash your hair before school because today is the day Riley comes back from his two-week vacation in Cuba.

We'll discuss Riley later.

"Be prepared for note launch right after the announcements," Susannah whispers, giving my clean hair the thumbs-up. "*Major* news."

I pour her an extra-big handful of chips and wink. "Launch from the right. My left arm hurts from wrestling with Gram's childproof vitamin jar."

Her mouth tightens into a little ball. "I promise you this—if I ever get offered a vitamin commercial, I'll refuse to do it on the grounds of injuries like yours. You should sue." She slides her sunglasses farther up her nose and swoops on past.

Let me explain about the dark glasses. When

Susannah was eight, she decided to become a World-Famous Child Star. Her mother thought it was an awesome idea, because everyone knows that World-Famous Child Stars' mothers have nice cars and extra-slim thighs. So Mrs. Barnes got all these pictures taken of her daughter and Susannah got an agent—

which is a special person who makes sure you get famous and get acting jobs and get to sign autographs. Sort of like the elephant keeper at the zoo on our third-grade field trip. He got the elephant all shined up and trained, and then took him out to get looked at and photographed by the public. Only, the elephant got paid in peanuts and Susannah got real coin.

Anyway, the agent's office is right above the doughnut shop, so every time Susannah has a meeting, she gets a Boston cream.

Lucky.

In about three seconds **Susannah got hired to do a real commercial,** and we celebrated by having a sleepover with five girls and a cake decorated with a movie camera made of icing. Then Susannah found out **the bad part.** The commercial that would make her world famous was about bed-wetting.

Bed-wetting!

It's obvious, of course, but I'll say it anyway: if you're planning to be a World-Famous Child Star, the last thing you want to be famous for is wetting the bed.

But Susannah did the commercial, because her Mom said, "It's money in the bank," and she hasn't taken off the glasses since. Which is kind of dumb since we all know it's her. Also, she hasn't gone to the bathroom at school ever since, just to prove that she, unlike the character she played, has one mighty ferocious bladder.

Riley is next in line, and because he's a show-off, but a very cute show-off, he spins and then leans down on my desk real close. **Riley Sinclair doesn't know it yet, but he's the boy I'm going to marry.**

The trouble is, I never get to see him after school. He has to practice, he always says. And I always say, "Practice what?" And he always says sumo wrestling, which I happen to know is a major lie, since Riley isn't remotely fat and doesn't like being seen in a bathing suit any shorter than his knees.

Once I had a boyfriend I saw every day after school. Guy. Pronounced like Key, but with a G. And no last name. Well, probably he had a last name, but I never knew it, since I was about five and what five-year-old knows anyone's last name? Guy was in my kindergarten class, and he used to call me on the phone every night and teach me how to say swearwords in French.

Ooh-la-la.

Anyway, Riley, who is not French but is still ooh-la-la, is wearing rumpled jeans and a shirt all shredded at the bottom from his falling off his skateboard. Also, his hair keeps flopping in his eye. He looks perfect, so that's what I start to tell him—

Suddenly Mrs. Patinkin, our language-arts teacher, glides in. "Good morning, scholars! Please take your seats. Are your minds open and ready to receive what the week has to offer?"

No one says it, since it would make Mrs. Patinkin cry, **but I guarantee we** *all* **think it. No!**

Somebody must have nodded or scratched themselves, because Mrs. Patinkin claps her hands and says, "Good. Let's begin by copying this inspirational quote I found in the Sunday paper. It incorporates three of last week's vocabulary words—*monarchy*, *pedicure*, and *canine*."

As she turns to write the inspirational quote on the board, I quickly tap Riley with a handful of chips. "You look exceptionally perfect—"

"Ahem. Zoë Monday Costello?" says Mrs. Patinkin.

Okay, so there *might* be a little

more to this Monday thing than I've admitted to. But I'm twelve years old now. I'm way past asking why a perfectly intelligent mother would saddle her only child with a middle name of the *one* day of the week everyone can't stand. **I sure must have kicked and screamed a lot on my way out to make my mother that mad.**

I swipe all the hair accessories and chocolate chips into my desk and sit up tall. Well, as tall as I can.

Mrs. Patinkin smiles. "Would you mind enlightening the rest of the class as to the topic of your private conversation?"

She's faking like she's punishing me—to show the others it's wrong to whisper during class—but she and I both know it's a big act. She really *wants* to know what I whisper about.

I smile to show her I don't mind in the least, and stand up. "Mrs. Patinkin," I say. People *love* to hear the sound of their own names. **"I was simply informing my classmate that inspiring students is the hallmark of a great teacher."**

A slow smile spreads across Mrs. Patinkin's face. For a moment she doesn't speak. Then she takes a deep breath.

"You see, class? It *is* possible to use our vocabulary words in real life. It's encouraging to see some students can reap the benefits of learning words like *hallmark.* Thank you, Zoë."

Mrs. Patinkin has a big thing about expanding our lousy vocabularies. She also has a big thing about saying the word *reap* and a very, very big thing **about extra-small people who are extra slippery with compliments.** She also has a very big thing about Stewie Buckenheimer going through the—

"Garbage!" Mrs. Patinkin says. "How many times have I told you, Stewie Alan Buckenheimer, to leave the trash can alone?"

"But I lost my retainer again!"

"Oh, Stewie." She sighs. "Didn't we agree, as a class, that what the dentist puts in our mouths stays in our mouths?"

"My gums were itchy." Stewie pulls his arm out of the trash can and by accident dumps the whole thing onto the floor. A puddle of liquid oozes toward Mrs. Patinkin's desk.

Mrs. Patinkin closes her eyes. She tries really hard not to

be the screamer type, but it's not always possible with a class like ours. So every time someone drives her into the danger zone, she does this little meditation thing afterward, where she shuts her eyes and tries to pretend we're not here. I once asked her what she thinks about when she's trying to erase our rottenness from her mind, because if it were me I'd be thinking of three things, in the following order:

1. Chocolate chips.
2. Horses with snow on their muzzles.
3. The way Riley looks when he gets water all over his chin at the drinking fountain and wipes it away with his sleeve.

Mrs. Patinkin told me she thinks about absolutely nothing. But, honestly, I think that's a lie. I tried it once, when Jamie Savage shared my seat on the bus. It was one of those dripping, melting early spring days—too winterish for sneakers, too springish for mittens—and Jamie had one boot resting on his other knee while he drummed some crummy song on his ankle. Big clods of dirty snow dripped from the bottom of his boot, and I had to move my backpack out of the way or risk total backpack rot.

That's when he did it.

Took his grubby little finger, **scraped a clump of slush off the bottom of his boot, and licked it.**

I scrunched up my face against the window and thought as hard as I could about absolutely nothing. But it didn't work.

Now Mrs. Patinkin's eyes are open again, and she's smiling and pressing her fingertips together like a spider doing squats on a mirror. She says, "Let's pull out a crisp, clean sheet of paper and a sharpened pencil, shall we? We'll write down five sentences about what life showed us this weekend. Then each and every one of us will share our own unique and magical voyage. Try to incorporate one of the new vocabulary words written on the chalkboard." She taps the list with her wooden pointer. "We've got fifteen minutes, starti-i-ing now."

Stewie puts his hand up. "You said 'we.' Does that mean you're going to tell us about your unique and magical voyage, too, Mrs. Patinkin?"

"No, Stewie. I was simply speaking collectively to show you we're all traveling on this journey together."

Sylvia Smye stands up, crawling in cowlicks. "My mother says I won't be going on any class trips until I'm sixteen because of the wickedness of today's society." She sits down and folds her hands on her desk.

Mrs. Patinkin's eyes are closed again. "Thank you, Sylvia."

Up goes Brianna Simpson's hand. "Mrs. Patinkin, is it okay if we use mechanical pencils?"

"That will be fine, Brianna."

Up goes Brianna's hand again. "Mrs. Patinkin, is it okay if my sheet of paper doesn't have three holes in it? Because I ran out."

Mrs. Patinkin looks up at the clock. **She's not thinking about nothing. She's thinking about 3:15.** "Yes, Brianna."

It turns out to be the quickest fifteen minutes ever, because she tells us to put down our sharpened pencils and read out loud, starting with the vocabulary word of our choice. I'm only halfway through my third sentence and still haven't even figured out how to work in the word mutilate.

Riley reads first. He reads real fast and doesn't stop for a breath until he's done, because he hates reading out loud. "Myvocabularywordis*blister*.ThisweekendIwentshopping forweddinggownswithmyoldestsister.Shetriedonthir-

teenpuffygowns,whichshesaidallmadeherlookfat.Isaidit
wasprobablyagoodthingshe'sgettingfat*before*theweddingso
herhusbandhasachancetochangehismindbeforeit'stoolate.
Shesaidshe'snevergettingmarriednowandcriedandcalled
meaLittleBlister.Thenthesaladygotallmadandmadeus
leavebecausemysister'smakeupgotcriedalloverthedresses."

Mrs. Patinkin looks confused. Then she says, "Wonderful, Riley. Harrison Huxtable, it's your turn."

The whole class laughs and a few people snort like little pigs. Mrs. Patinkin swats at them in the air.

It takes Harrison Huxtable a minute to stand up. He seems to have his thigh wedged between his desk and his chair. By the time he gets fully upright, the kids are howling. This is not acceptable. Harrison cannot help it, and besides, **nobody who can draw perfectly shaded birds of prey like Harrison can should ever have to suffer torment from complete losers.** I spin around and hiss at the hecklers and they finally cut it out.

Morons.

"My name is Harrison Huxtable. My word is *luncheon*. On the weekend my family had a garage sale. I sold my old bicycle, which was broken, and my old computer chair, which was also broken. I made 15 dollars but I had to miss luncheon. Thank you."

Mrs. Patinkin claps her hands because the morons are laughing again. I stomp my foot and glare until the class shuts up.

"Not quite the proper use of the word," says Mrs. Patinkin. "But thank you, Mr. Huxtable. It sounds like you're turning into a real titan of industry."

Harrison Huxtable looks pretty pleased about that part. He sits down and beams pure pink.

"Laurel, you can go next."

Laurel stands up, nearly blinding us all with her colors. She reads, "My vocabulary word is *stupendous*. My title is 'My Weekend, by Laurel Sterling.' " She pauses to cough. "I had a perfectly stupendous time. First, I organized my sock drawer. Then I told my sister to keep her hairy, half-dead cat away from my beanbag chair or all the popcorn will pour out and she'll have to buy me a new one. And I happen to know the store's all out. I was supposed to go to a birthday party, but changed my mind. That is the story of my stupendous weekend. Stupendous."

Someone at the back laughs and calls out, "Why didn't you go? Was the cake the wrong color?"

Laurel sits down and covers her face, which is getting more colorful than her sweater. Laurel cries sometimes. It gets to be too much for her, all the problems about the blue food. It's why she needs me.

I spin around to find Martin Granitstein snickering. **"Why don't you shut your sticky face, Smartin!"** I say.

"Zoë," says Mrs. Patinkin. Great. I slump down in my chair. See? You try to defend the masses—or even just your number two BFIS—and what happens? You are publicly shamed. Stripped of your dignity. **This is the kind of thing that makes me seriously reevaluate my entire Lama career.** I mean, Mrs. Patinkin is not and never will be a Lama herself, but I'd hoped she would know enough not to be dragged over to the dark side by defending Smartin, of all people! Why should I go to all the trouble—for no pay, I might add—if those in semileadership positions can't even see the self-sacrifice?

Seriously?

Mrs. Patinkin continued. "Mr. Granitstein is on his way to Principal Renzetti's office. And while I'm quite certain he knows the way, would you mind delivering the attendance book to Mrs. Delaney at the front desk? That way we can be sure Martin won't get 'lost,' like he did last week." Smartin groans and starts dragging his feet toward the door.

Oh. Never mind.

I shove the baggie into my pocket and stand up. **If I have to walk in the shadow of the Beast, at least I'm doing it with chocolate.**

Mrs. Patinkin stops me when I'm halfway out the door. "Zoë, wait." She shuffles to the doorway and leans closer to me. Then she smoothes out her purple stirrup pants and her shaggy sweater and whispers, "For Picture Day . . . is this suitable?"

It isn't, but I'm a girl who knows the right side from the wrong side of a teacher's red pen. "It's hot, Mrs. Patinkin," I lie, and spin around.

*T*he office is full of gym coaches yelling at basketball players, parents bringing forgotten lunch boxes, and fifth-grade babies getting their bruises iced. And while I'd like to deliver Smartin and then bolt for the sweet smell of a hallway without Smartin in it, I have to sit on a bench outside of Principal Renzetti's office and wait until his secretary, Gladys Stitt, gets off the phone to hand off my revolting delivery, who is starting to stink like blue cheese. I slide to the farthest end of the bench, stick two chocolate chips together by licking the bottoms, and plop them onto my tongue. If I don't suck too fast, I figure I have enough chips to last me until Gladys finishes ordering her new curtains *and* her throw pillows.

I never said it was easy being me. Not that I can't handle this or anything, but **some days the load is heavier—and smellier—than others.**

My friends I'll deal with, since, really, what other option do I have? Without me, they'd still be playing with electronic puppies and laughing at knock-knock jokes. And the teachers I put up with for reasons of self-preservation and eventual college acceptance. You can never think too long-term. The pill-swallowing grandma, well, she's the closest thing I've got to my dad, so I never complain about her.

It's Mom. I could handle everything else if she only had some kind of helper. Then I'd never have to worry, did she forget the milk again? Is she late for work and going to get fired? That's exactly what **Mom needs . . . an assistant.**

Grandma's getting too old for the job. It's not really fair to ask a seventy-five-year-old lady to hand-wash your

Garage Girls T-shirt so the glitter doesn't wear off, and I never get all the soap out. Mom needs a husband. Just think of it—two adults to do all the work! If one forgets to pick up butter, the other one chirps, "That's okay, honey. I'll get it on my way home!"

And when Grandma makes a huge mess in the kitchen by dropping her applesauce jar on the floor, there'd be no more "Zoë, can you grab a few towels and mop up? Watch out for the broken glass." No way. That would be the assistant's job. I'd be too busy drawing in my room or talking Laurel through Christmas dinner on the phone.

Life would be perfect.

As I balance a chocolate chip on my nose, Mr. Lindsay, the math teacher, walks into the office hallway and thumbtacks a pink poster to the bulletin board. At the top, it says,

VOLUNTEERS NEEDED FOR WINTER DANCE COMMITTEE

Anyone up for a challenge and a laugh?

Sign up below!

A pen taped to a long string hangs from the poster.

Mr. Lindsay would make a pretty good assis-

tant for my mother. He's always got important-looking math tools in his shirt pocket, and he sure put up that poster nice and straight. Plus, **his face isn't completely hideous.**

Scrubbing my hands on my jeans, I jump up and write Zoë Costello on the first line. I'm definitely up for a challenge and a laugh. Can I help it if it happens to get my mom a husband and me more time for *The Garage Girls*? I think not.

You Can Step in a Load of Crap, but a Smart Girl Doesn't Put Up with Any

When I was seven, I discovered that eating spinach wasn't ever going to give me bulging muscles, like my mother had always told me. Which meant **she'd been lying to me my whole life.** And that got me thinking about her lying about other stuff. Like my irritating cousin Risa really being related to me and my dad dying when I was little. If a woman could fake out her own kid about being able to lift a car off an injured squirrel by eating another forkful of drippy green leaves, then she's probably capable of lying about the bigger stuff.

I figured, since **I couldn't remember much about Dad** and in his photos he looks exactly like the undershirt model from the Wal-Mart flyers, that maybe him dying was a hoax, too. And that **maybe he was actually alive and well and working at Wal-Mart.** In the underwear section.

I never said I was a brilliant seven-year-old.

Then I overheard Mom talking to a neighbor, who said, "If I could do it all over again, I'd marry a plastic surgeon." Then Mom laughed and said, "You and me both." Which, I thought, was maybe her motive all along—to kill him off in my mind by leaving him at Wal-Mart one day while she went looking for the guy with the age-scraping knife.

So I copied the Wal-Mart address from the phone book and wrote Dad a long letter, telling him about how I can wiggle my ears and how I just learned to do a one-handed cartwheel in gymnastics class. I also told him how my favorite picture is the one he took of me sitting on the steps of our secret place. The one not even Mom knows about— the Hunters Park gazebo where he took me the night we flushed my dead goldfish down the toilet. Dad's not in the picture, but I still remember him taking it, laughing because snowflakes kept landing on the camera lens.

It's the one Dad memory I have.

I also told him Mom didn't have much luck marrying any kind of doctor at all. Then I thought I should include a gift, so before I licked the envelope, I stuck in the twenty-dollar bill I got for my birthday in case he felt like buying chocolate chips or a pair of hip waders.

Then I wrote my address on the front of the envelope and on the back, just in case some dirt got smeared on the front and he couldn't read it. Because he might want to thank me for the money. Or ask if it hurts my hand to do a one-handed cartwheel. He might even want me to give Mom a special message from him.

You never know.

For two months after that, I made sure to look through the mail before anyone else did. I didn't want Mom to find his letter before I got to tell him the cartwheel only hurts my hand when I do it on very hot pavement or the gravelly sidewalk beside the library.

Only I never got to tell him, since **his letter never came.**

A little while after that, when Mom was in a really good mood because Grandma slept in, I asked her if she could take me to Wal-Mart. When we got there, **I faked a stomachache beside the men's underwear section, hoping my dad would come running** out from behind a stack of tube socks to save the day. Only he didn't. A short little woman with an accent came instead, and when she bent over me her glasses swung down from a chain and hit me in the eyelid. But what hurt more than that was when I asked her who else worked in her department and she said, "Nobody." It had been her and only her for years.

It really just goes to show: when I was seven, I was a real dope.

After I leave Smartin in the office with a stern warning we both know he'll ignore, I head back to language arts with an empty baggie in my pocket and speed in my step. We're scheduled to go for pictures in half an hour and I haven't finger-combed Ingrid's bangs yet.

"*Psst!* Zoë Lama."

I spin around to see Annika Pruitt from eighth grade hiding behind the door to the girls' restroom. Her gigantic head of red wavy hair is so thick it's practically holding the door open by itself.

I stop. "Hey."

She waves me to come inside, so I do. **I don't mind helping the eighth graders, not really.** It's kind of flattering to be asked to advise older girls, but Annika is a bit needy. She's always "tragically wounded" from regular things people say, like: "Annika, you dropped your sandwich," or "Annika, your sleeve is stuck in the door," or "Annika, those aren't winter gloves, they're oven mitts."

I wouldn't ever want to tell her she has spinach in her teeth.

"Zoë. You won't believe it," she says, yanking me inside. "Justin Rosetti walked me to school today and you won't believe it!"

I bet I will. Justin's a toad. "Spill."

"We were almost at school when there was this sick, steaming pile of fresh dog you-know-what, and Justin drops my hand and jumps out of the way and I end up stepping in it. Some boyfriend." She gets teary. "And what's even worse, look at my new shoes!" She lifts one up and shows me the packed-tight mass of putrid-osity that is now her sole.

And her soul.

"Okay," I say. I actually feel bad for her this time. Justin's a dork and does not deserve a girl with this much hair. "Pull the shoe off; **I'm pretty good with poop**." I turn on the hot-water tap to form a shallow lake in the sink, then pour in about fourteen gallons of soap. "The thing is, Annika, you can step in a load of crap, anyone can. But a smart girl doesn't put up with any. Ever. **It's an Unwritten Rule. Number six, to be exact.**"

"Unwritten Rule? Cool. Where do I get a copy of these Unwritten Rules? Is there a rule book?"

Should I really have to explain this? I sigh and say, **"The rules are *unwritten*. There is no rule book. If they were in a rule book, they wouldn't be unwritten."**

Annika grins. "So, what you're saying is they're invisible."

"You could say that."

"Why don't you call them Invisible Rules? I like that better."

I grit my teeth. "Because they're *my* rules, so *I* get to name them."

With this, she jumps up and squeezes me so hard I get bubbles (thankfully clean bubbles) all the way up to my elbows. "Whatever they're called, thanks!" she squeals.

*B*ack in the hall I break into a run. I may be dripping from both arms, but I'm *not* missing Picture Day. I cut through the fifth-grade hallway to save time and realize, too late, that **a gaggle of balloons is coming straight at me.** It seems to be attached to a gigantic birthday cake with legs.

I spin and race back the way I came, checking to see if the balloon cake is following me. Spotting an open janitor's closet, I dive inside, slam the door, and collapse on top of a mop that stinks of pinecones.

That was close!

I have a tiny secret. No one else on the Entire Planet knows it except my family and a certain balloon-making clown at the beach last year. But the doctor said the scratches wouldn't scar his face and I should just forget the whole ugly incident.

I'm terrified of balloons.

I know they don't roar or have teeth or claws or anything, but I despise them with passion. And for a small person I have an awful lot of passion at my disposal.

You never know what to expect from a balloon. They could pop at any moment and *bang!* you go deaf. Or worse, a popped piece could hit your eye like a missile and take it right out. Then you're half blind. Unless you only had one eye to begin with, and then you're fully blind. Or you could accidentally swallow a small one and forever have it lodged in your intestines. And then there're the ones little kids have tied to their wrists, ones that blow all around in the wind and bop you in the face when you're standing nearby, innocently trying to eat your ice-cream cone. And don't even talk to me about hot-air balloons. Dangling in a wicker basket hundreds of feet above the ground with nothing more than a crappy balloon to keep you from plunging to a cruel demise isn't exactly my idea of a rockin' time.

The possibilities for disaster are endless with balloons—this is Unwritten Rule #1.

There's nothing cool about a balloon anxiety in seventh grade. Other anxieties, like Fear of Cappuccino or Fear of Stepping in Potholes—these fears are cute and quirky and highly desirable. Part of growing up an innocent victim of the big city. *Very* popularity boosting.

Fear of Balloons, on the other hand, ranks right up there with Fear of Losing Your Mommy at the A&P or Fear of Giant Purple Dinosaurs.

Cracking the door open, I poke my head out into the hall. Looks clear, but I better not risk fifth-grader land again. Those babies are still too fascinated with inflatables. I head back around the office to see Smartin squashing his face against the window to the hallway. He's puffing up his cheeks like a particularly ugly pig-nosed blowfish.

I screech to a stop at Mrs. Patinkin's classroom and burst inside.

The whole class is silent. And they look worried. When I get to my desk I realize why. **There's someone sitting at it and she's definitely not me!**

"Hi. You're at my desk," I say.

The squatter looks up and smiles. "Sorry, Zoë." Then she holds out a handful of barrettes with a few chocolate chips mixed in. "I think these are yours."

"Maisie Robbins is new to the school," says Mrs. Patinkin. "So go ahead and take a seat, Zoë."

I look up. Do I have to say it? "I don't have a—"

"Right there at the back, next to Martin's desk."

Ugh. It doesn't get any worse than sitting next to Smartin. As I trudge back, I pass Susannah, who tips her glasses and smiles sadly. Then I pass Laurel, who punches me twice, our secret punch for sympathy. Then comes the worst part. I pass Riley and realize, from this moment on, **I might as well be moving to the opposite end of the world.** Because that's how far I'll be from the boy I'm going to marry.

The farther back I go, the worse it gets. The air seems to thicken. The ground seems to sway. I pass Harrison

Huxtable, who winks and smiles, and then I pass Avery's smeary glasses. Oh no. There's one empty seat with a stack of all my worldly possessions piled on the desk, and it's squashed right behind Avery, and between Smartin and Alice, whose vest is *infested* with prancing kittens. That girl's clothing needs to be spayed. Or neutered, depending.

It's a moron colony back here.

Just then, a note launch comes in from the northwest. I catch it easily and uncrumple it. It just so happens to be from **the most unbelievably cute guy in school**, or the **MUCGIS**.

> To my favorite Backie,
> Don't be sad. Think about how much you've helped us Fronties. Don't the Backies deserve the same? Just don't forget us when the chocolate chip bag is full.
> Riley Sinclair
> P.S. Remember to use your power for good, not evil.

o o o

That's another thing about Riley. He's a very good sort of person. Sometimes, I think, far too good for the sort of girl who complains as much as I do. He likes it when I help people, but he gets grumbly when I go too far. Like the time I told Sylvia she should think about dyeing her hair bright red to take the focus off her cowlicks.

Riley said, "You're stomping all over her self-esteem!"

But I said, "No! It's just like redecorating. Like throwing a really pretty blanket over a lumpy old couch."

"So now you're calling Sylvia a lumpy old couch?" he asked.

I just patted his cheek. Poor guy. He missed the whole point. Which, obviously, was the really pretty blanket.

I look up now to see Riley smiling at me from the front. **Now I feel worse. Suddenly I'm a Backie** and no longer even in the same category as my number one and number two BFIS or the MUCGIS.

I slump down in my new chair, which is really more of a stool, since the back is broken off. It's strangely tall, so my feet don't even hit the floor when I swing my legs. They just dangle back and forth like a toddler on a bus. Not only that, but **the smell of Smartin lingers on and on**.

I raise my hand.

Mrs. Patinkin smiles at me, looking genuinely sorry. "Your desk was closest to the blackboard, Zoë. Maisie has depth-perception problems and will reap the benefits of sitting up front. **Now, are we all ready to conjugate the verb** *suffer*?"

I swing my legs and the back of my knee gets pinched in a crack in the chair seat. At least there's no blood. I guess the lack of blood makes me smile or nod or something, which Mrs. Patinkin takes as an answer that, yes, I am ready to conjugate. Even though I'm *so* not.

"Good. We'll make it a pop quiz, just for fun."

So not.

You Can't Polish a Poodle

By the time I get on the city bus, almost every seat is taken either by kids on their way home from school or by adults who probably wish they had earplugs. Unless I want to sit beside the frazzled lady with the whiny triplets, and I so don't, **I'm stuck with Harrison Huxtable**, which is bad because he's playing **with his yo-yo** and the minute I sit down he starts letting it "sleepwalk" into my ankle.

"I'm going to be in a professional competition," he says. "Yo-Yo-Palooza. It's in March. Remember how you told me to practice, practice, practice, and one day it'd pay off?"

"Sort of."

"It worked. **Want me to show you how I Walk the Dog?**"

I smile and shake my head no. "I'm not really in the mood right now. . . ."

"Okay, here goes," he says, and winds the string up. Only he has to stop a few times because his fingers get wrapped up, too, and then he has to stop to detangle. Once he's finally free, he smacks his gum and grins. "Ready?"

I smile and shake my head no.

"Okay, here goes," he says, and flings the yo-yo down until it smacks against the floor and, no longer spinning, bobs and twirls at the end of the string while he moves his hand to the right. "See? That's Walk the Dog."

I think it's Kill the Dog, but I just smile and raise my eyebrows to show him I'm impressed. And just when I'm thinking how lucky everyone is that I don't always say what I'm really thinking, the bus stops and someone calls out, **"Hey, look at that old nutcase!"** and the whole bus rocks with kids' laughter.

I scramble over Harrison Huxtable's giant lunch box and mash my face into the window. By the time I realize what I'm looking at, the bus starts to pull away.

But not before I see what I really did *not* want to see. And that's **a little old lady** charging down Allencroft Boulevard toward the school. Nice red purse. Granny glasses hanging on a chain. **No big deal.**

Wearing fuzzy pink footsie pajamas. Outside. On the street. In the middle of the afternoon. **Very big deal.**

Especially when it's your grandma. Or, more specifically, *my* **grandma!**

She must be coming to pick me up. Like she used to. Since Mom worked, Grandma always met me at school and walked me home to keep me safe from, you know, twisted strangers. She came to meet me right up until the last day of fifth grade, which was more than a little embarrassing since I was the only fifth-grader with her own security. But Mom said until I was too big for a twisted stranger to stuff into a backpack, I was busing it with a bodyguard.

So **how did Gram forget that she hasn't picked me up in a year and a half?**

Worse, **how did she forget to get dressed?**

Harrison explodes laughing. His yo-yo falls to the ground and rolls under the seat. "She's wearing footsie pajamas outside!" he shouts. "Just like mine, only pink!"

This has an instant happy-sad effect. Happy for me, because the bloodthirsty wolves in the seats behind me instantly go after Harrison's flesh and bones instead of Grandma's. Sad, because Harrison just offered himself up as roadkill.

A seventh-grade boy admitting to wearing footsies is so socially taboo it doesn't even need an Unwritten Rule.

I jump up and pull the cord to signal to the driver that I need to get off. Fast. Thankfully, the next stop is around the corner, so none of the wolves can see me tearing back to find Grandma and take her home.

 B ack at home that night, Mom pours dry rice into a pot of boiling water. Steam spills out and hides her face for a moment. "I'm going to have to ask you to sort through the laundry hamper after dinner. Grandma lost her teeth and I don't want them going through the dryer again."

I stick a wooden spoon into the pot and drown the rice bits that are swimming on the surface.

"Mom?"

"Yes?"

"When people get old and start forgetting things, do they also start doing crazy stuff? Sometimes in public?"

She looks at me funny. "Yes. Sometimes. Especially if they have Alzheimer's."

"What's that?" I ask.

"It's when older people's minds age quicker than their bodies."

"Mm." I stir the rice around the pot and stare at the bubbling water. "What do their families do about Alzheimer's?"

"Mostly just try to cope. And when it gets to the point that the older person needs constant care, **their families often put them into a nursing home**. So they'll be safe and well cared for."

Not my grandma. Not in my lifetime. I study my mother's face. "We'd never do that, would we? To Grandma?"

She pauses too long, then puts the box of rice back into the cupboard. "If it became necessary, we'd consider it."

I don't like that answer. Or that pause. And I especially don't like the word *Alzheimer's*.

Grandma is like my rock. Nothing blows her over, makes her wilt or melt away. After Dad died, Mom spent a lot of time in bed sniffling, so Grandma moved in to "set things straight." And she *so* did.

I remember coming home from kindergarten one spring day and all these suitcases were piled up in the hallway. I didn't know who belonged to them, but they looked like a good fort, so I dumped my backpack on the floor and crawled inside. Just as I was pretending to feed my wolf-cub children, Grandma's face poked in and said, "Boo!" Which was scary but good, since I hadn't seen Grandma in a long time and she always smells like baby powder and hugs.

"Grandma!" I shouted as I trampled over my cubs to kiss her cheek. I knocked over the whole pile of suitcases, but Grandma didn't mind. She just said, "That's what luggage is for," and scooped me up in her arms.

Grandma moved in that day. Suddenly we had hot meals on the table, laundry folded and put away, and, lots of times, warm and chewy chocolate-chip cookies on the kitchen counter when I got home from school.

I've never even *known* **anyone smarter than Grandma.** She used to talk on and on about baseball stuff, like whose batting average was .375 and whose ERA was 1.79. I didn't know what she was talking about; it was just fun to listen. And crossword puzzles—that was the best part. **Every Sunday morning we used to sit and do the crossword in the newspaper until we finally got fed up, ripped it into tiny shreds, and made cocoa.** I always got fed up first, so I got pretty good at making cocoa.

"I hear some nursing homes are quite chichi these days," Mom says now. "Big rooms, high-definition TV, spectacular views. You'll probably put me in one someday."

"Are you kidding? **I'd never lock** *you* **up.**"

"It's not prison, Zoë. Some nursing homes are very nice."

"Who takes care of these old people—the ones whose families don't want them?"

"Nurses. And their families don't 'not want them.' "

"Can they leave if they want to—these old people?"

"Well, no. But—"

"Then **it's prison and Grandma's never going.**"

She squints at me and pours a glass of milk. "Did something happen to Grandma today, Zoë? Is there something I should know about?"

"Nope," I lie. **"It was a perfectly normal day."** Once I'm satisfied there are no survivors, I smother the steaming rice pot with a lid, turn down the heat, and set the timer for twenty-five minutes.

Just then Grandma's footsies come swish-swishing into the kitchen. She sits at the table and lifts her feet onto an empty chair. She pulls a tissue from her bathrobe pocket and blows her nose before picking up a pen and eyeballing this morning's crossword puzzle. "That **Alex Trebek** from *Jeopardy!* **is a ninny**," she says, scribbling down an answer. "On television for the whole world to see and he's not even wearing a tie today."

I stare at a clod of gum stuck to her pajama footsies and say nothing.

The phone rings.

"Zoë, will you put the chicken on a plate, please?" Mom asks, picking up the phone. Covering the receiver with her hand, she rolls her eyes and whispers to me, "It's the office, you'll have to take over. Try to pull off the skin before you slice the chicken, it's easier on Gram's stomach." She goes back to her phone call and rubs her forehead with her hand. "Francine lost the Fullerton contracts?"

Here we go again. I don't know why this Francine chick is given any responsibilities at all, because Mom's always having to swoop in and cover for her. I guess it's because Francine is a single mom with three kids and Mom doesn't want to fire her and be responsible for a bunch of kids having no food and no roof over their heads.

"But why was she bringing the contracts with her to Toddler Splash?" Mom asks. She's frantically digging through her purse now.

I slice some skin off the chicken and notice little sharp things sticking out. Then I realize that this bird doesn't even have all its feathers pulled out yet. "Gross! This chicken's still alive; I'm not touching it!"

Mom shushes me and whispers, "Just pull off the skin, Zoë!" Then she turns away. "Are you sure all three copies went under?"

"It's too revolting," I say, dropping the knife onto the counter. "I feel like a murderer! Grandma, can you do it?"

"Give it a try," Grandma says. "Just catch the feather shafts between your fingernails and yank."

"Disgusting! I can't do this!"

Grandma shakes her head, stands up, and shuffles slowly toward me. Then she takes the knife from my hand and drops it onto the counter. The blade spins around to face me. **Gleaming metal pointing directly at a kid's knuckles seems like the kind of thing that should bother an adoring, sane grandma, doesn't it?** Well, it isn't bothering mine.

I decide my fingers might be safer in my pockets, so I stuff them there—fast. Then she says, "It's simple. Watch me." Just like she said, **she rips out the broken feathers,** one by one, **and tosses them onto the counter, where I can look at them and try really hard not to heave.**

I cover my mouth. "Ugh."

Grandma swipes the feather stems into her hand and drops them into the trash, smiling at me. All of a sudden she seems like an incredibly adoring, sane grandma. I mean, anyone who can pluck broken-off feather stems with their bare hands and not even come *close* to vomiting has to be pretty solid, right?

Then she looks at me, shakes her head, and sighs. "One of these days I guess I'll learn **you just can't polish a poodle.**"

Polish a poodle? I glance at Mom real quick, relieved to see she didn't hear Grandma. One thing's certain. I'm going to have to cover for Grandma. **Talk like that could definitely get her locked up.**

Even Bad Reputations Need Expiration Dates

"So anyway," I say with a mouthful of apple.

It's recess. The early November sky is dark gray and I think I see a few snowflakes blowing around. It wasn't supposed to be this cold today, so I'm wearing a thin red Windbreaker that is actually doing a rotten job of breaking up the wind. "What was your major news yesterday?"

Susannah pushes her sunglasses higher up her perfect nose and pulls a hood over her head until all that's left of her face is her nose and glasses. **It's like talking to the Grim Reaper, only without the sickle.** She pulls Laurel and me closer to the brick wall and whispers, "I knew all about this new girl coming. Maisie."

Laurel snorts. I don't think she meant to make an actual snort, but it comes out that way. "That's major news? It isn't even news anymore. She's already here."

"So she showed up a day too early. It was news at the time."

"Still," Laurel says. Then she makes eyeglasses with her

hands so she looks like Susannah. "A new kid is coming! A new kid is coming!" She laughs. "It's not that newsworthy, that's all I'm saying."

Mostly, Laurel and Susannah are pretty solid BFIS number twos to each other. But **there's a tiny amount of ... tension between them that bubbles up.** It's been going on for a long time now, and it's a very delicate situation that I try very hard to ignore.

People assume it's because they both put me in their number one BFIS slot. That could certainly cause stress. And everyone thinks Laurel is jealous of Susannah's number one spot with me. Which may or may not be true. But these aren't the real reasons behind the on-again, off-again tension.

Sadly, Laurel used to be a bed-wetter. So when Susannah got the commercial, Laurel was glad. Finally, she thought, someone is going to bring bed-wetting out from under the sheets. A beautiful girl is going to announce to the world that she wets the bed and then it will become, if not cool, then at the very least not quite so embarrassing.

That was what Laurel had *hoped*. Of course it didn't happen that way. Susannah, who can be a teensy bit insensitive, moaned and groaned about not wanting people to think she was a bed-wetter and went into perma-hiding. It kind of enraged Laurel.

And just about the time when Laurel outgrew her nighttime problem, **Susannah landed her second commercial,** which aired last year. This one was even worse than bed-wetting. **It was for sanitary pads.** By the time Laurel finished giggling about the humiliation Susannah would face, not only had the commercial aired, but Susannah was known across the country for having become "A Woman." Her schoolwide fame reached dazzling new heights and **she had to get even bigger sunglasses.** Whether she'd started her period or not (she had, but I'll never tell!), we all knew Susannah was miles more mature than the rest of us.

Laurel still hasn't gotten over Susannah's comeback. And who can blame her? As of yesterday, she's still the only girl in seventh grade to not have her period.

Nature can be so cruel.

Suddenly someone near the baseball diamond screams, **"GIRL FIGHT!"** and hordes of kids race over from every which direction. By the time we get there, they're chanting, "Fight! Fight! Fight!" We push past a group of GameWizard boys, better known as Lame Wizards, and nose our way in front of the basketball chicks to find two fifth-grade girls, bundled up in puffy pastel coats, colored tights, and sheepskin boots, whacking the stars out of each other with pretty woolen hats.

It's like a fight between two muppets.

The one with neon-pink braces pushes the other one down onto her back, hollering, "Leave us alone!" The whole school gets a peek at the purple bloomers she's wearing over her tights. Bloomer Girl then kicks out at Neon Pink's knobby knees but misses entirely. Poor Bloomer Girl's jacket is so padded she can't get any good traction. Somebody gives her a lift from behind and she runs full force into Neon Pink, knocking her straight into Mrs. Kettleby, the librarian.

"All right, show's over," Mrs. Kettleby says, grabbing the two of them by the mittens and prying them apart. "The rest of you go about your business while I straighten out these two."

"Well," Susannah says, kicking a ball toward some sixth-grade boys who aren't particularly good at playing foursquare, **"I happen to know more about Maisie than anyone else in the school."**

"Okay, spill," I command. Who knows? This might get juicy.

Susannah has been waiting for this moment. She lowers her glasses, looks around, then whispers, **"Her family used to rent a cottage near ours** on Lake Labrador every summer. Remember that guy, Nicholas, I used to talk about?"

Laurel pulls a blue juice pack from her pocket and punches a straw into it. Blue juice spurts out all over her coat, which, luckily, is blue. "Talk about? You scratched his name into the crabapple tree in my backyard. And the next year it didn't bloom."

"I don't remember that," Susannah says, checking her Grim Reaper hoodie for accidental blue squirts.

"My mother does," says Laurel.

Susannah says, "Anyway, back to me. It was the last year we were at the lake. **Nicholas was planning to take me for a canoe ride at sunset** and I packed some pâté and grapes I stole from my parents' dinner party. Right before I left, Maisie knocked on my door. She handed me a note, said it was from Nicholas, and disappeared."

"What did the note say?" I ask.

"It said he had to cancel. He was sorry and he hoped I enjoyed sixth grade."

"Bummer," says Laurel.

"But that's not the worst," says Susannah. "Later that week, I heard from my cousin that Maisie wrote the note herself and then gave him a note from *me*. It said something about me not wanting to expose my hair to the damp evening air." Susannah shakes her head. **"Everyone knew what she did.** Her Lake Labrador reputation was ruined."

"Why'd she do it?" asks Laurel.

"So she could go canoeing with Nicholas, who, naturally, was brokenhearted that I canceled."

"Wow. **The old bait and switch,"** I say, shivering and wrapping my waste of a Windbreaker tighter around me. Grandma used to say that when my mother dangled chocolate chips in front of me so I'd eat my lima beans.

Bloomer Girl runs past, being chased by Neon Pink, who's carrying a broken lunch box and screaming.

Laurel's eyebrows scrunched together. "The old what?"

I smile. "Nothing."

"The point is," Susannah continues, **"Maisie has a terrible reputation.** And a reputation follows you everywhere you go. Forever."

Don't I know it. **Another reason for balloons to be banished from society.** I zip my jacket to my chin.

Laurel points toward the side of the school where the bad kids hang out. "Look. There's Maisie now. How do you think she knows those bad girls already? **Are rotters just drawn to each other like magnets?**"

Maisie is laughing with Tara Smye, Sylvia's bigger, badder sister; Monica Granitstein, Smartin's bigger, just-as-bad older sibling; and Jessie Krutz, who once toilet-papered Principal Renzetti's Toyota. With twenty-seven double rolls. Quilted.

Suddenly I remember something. "How did you know Maisie was coming to our school if you haven't seen her since that summer?"

Susannah bugs her eyes. "My mother works with her mother. She had a bad reputation at her last school, too."

"So what exactly did Maisie do at her last school to earn her this reputation?" I ask.

"She's *mean.*"

"How mean?" asks Laurel.

"*Very* mean," Susannah says, arching her eyebrows. "She

has a reputation for being horrible, rotten, stinking mean."

Laurel laughs. "Kicked out of school for being mean? Principal Renzetti should have been tossed out years ago!"

"How do you know?" I ask Laurel. "You've never even spoken to Principal Renzetti!"

She fidgets with her coat collar and looks around. "I hear things."

At this point, something perfectly delicious happens. Riley Sinclair runs by and tugs on my hair. Then he turns around to face me and, walking backward, says, "Hey."

"Hey," I shout back. Then Riley runs off, because his friends are chasing him with a squirting water bottle.

It's weird what the littlest, nothingest "hey" can do to your whole day. **One tug on my hair and suddenly I'm beaming.** I've stopped shivering. The brats have stopped screaming. The sky is suddenly filled with swallows.

Then again, they could be buzzards. What do I know about birds?

Even Maisie and her reputation don't look so bad.

Neon Pink is walking backward now, pulling Bloomer Girl by her boots. Bloomer Girl almost looks like she's enjoying the ride until her right boot comes off, exposing a striped toe sock. Then she wails like a stray cat. Mrs. Kettleby comes trotting over again, waving a finger at Neon Pink, who takes off with the lavender boot.

We move away from the wildness while Mrs. Kettleby chases Neon Pink across the soccer field. Honestly, these babies should not be allowed in school until they're at least eleven. And a half.

I finish my apple and toss the core at the trash can, missing it by a mile. "You know what I'm thinking? **Maisie's fresh and new now.** No one but us knows of her past. She's done nothing mean here. Yet. So," I continue, picking up the core and depositing it properly, "we should consider her as having *no* reputation. Give her a clean slate."

"What?" says Susannah. "She already has a reputation here. Because I know all about her. And so do you. She walked right into the same reputation as ever."

"Even bad reputations need expiration dates. Let's dump hers down the sink."

"You can't dump it down the sink. It is what it is!"

"Not if we do the right thing. Dump it."

Laurel turns to me. "So, just like that, her old reputation is irreverent?"

Susannah and I look at each other.

"I think you mean irrelevant," I say. "'Irreverent' means disrespectful. Rude."

Laurel's cheeks get pink. "She sounds pretty rude to me!"

"A reputation can't be rude—" I stop myself. I don't have the energy. "But yes, just like that, her past is irrelevant." I glance over at Maisie, who is trying on Monica's shredded jean jacket. "I think she needs our help . . ."

"*Our* help?" Susannah and Laurel say together.

"We can't let her bury herself again. We may be her only chance."

"Well, good luck to you. I'm certainly not helping anybody who hangs out with Monica Granitstein," says Laurel.

"Me neither," Susannah says. **"I've been burned once by that girl.** Besides, my mother said to stay away from her."

"That's okay," I say as the bell rings. Kids everywhere scream and tear back toward the school doors like they're being chased by killer bees. Once they pass, all that remains are a few dozen granola-bar wrappers and one very fleecy, very lavender boot.

I walk across the pavement and pick it up. **"I can handle this on my own."**

$\mathcal{I}$t isn't until after school that I finally find Bloomer Girl. She's heading toward the parent parking lot wearing one beige sneaker and one lavender boot.

"Hey," I call out, not knowing her name and not wanting to depress her further by telling her I know about the bloomers. I catch up to her before she gets into her mother's Mercedes. She smiles when she sees the boot. "You found it!"

"Yeah. I tried to buff out some of the dried mud between classes. **It's a very nice boot. You must be proud."**

Taking her boot from me, she shrugs. This girl has the kind of haircut where the back is all short and choppy like a boy's and the front comes down to her chin. Like her hair is on backward. "I guess. Doesn't do me any good, though."

"What do you mean?"

"Nothing. Just that no one ever wants to hang out with me. That's what the fight was about. My parents told me to go up to a few girls and ask if I could hang out with them. I tried it a few times and, well, you saw what happened."

My instincts were correct. **Bloomer Girl is a good guy.** Which reminds me, "What's your name?"

"Allegra."

"Allegra. Pretty."

"Thanks. I don't want to take up your time. I know who you are. You're the Zoë Lama. You've got clients way more important than a stupid fifth-grader. But thanks for saving my boot."

Her mother beeps her horn and Allegra turns to get in. I grab her sleeve. "Wait a minute. You're just as important as my older clients. Here's what you do. **Never ask anyone to hang with you. It's needy and a turn-off.** You want to appear as if you're having a great time— all the time—and they'll come to you, begging to join in. Get it?"

Her mother calls, "Piano lessons, honey. We're going to be late."

She looks up. "I'm coming, Mom." Then she turns back to me. "Kind of . . ."

"Never beg for fun. Make your own fun and then sit back and let them beg to join in. **Find something funny in the playground and laugh your head off.** Notice something strange in the hallway and point it out. Don't be quiet either. Make sure you're heard. **Before you know it, they'll be crawling all over you.**"

A smile spreads across her little face and she leans down and hugs me tight. "Thank you, Zoë Lama. It's just like they say—you're the best!"

Never Argue When There's Candy at Stake

"Zoë!"

A gigantic beetle has just discovered me hiding under the kitchen sink. Only it's not our sink, which has broken baby-proof latches on the cupboard doors from when I was little so I didn't fill my sippy cup with Mr. Clean or something. Anyway, the beetle is horrifying and he's shining a flashlight right into my eyes, turning it on and off, on and off, on and off.

It's getting on my nerves, actually.

"Zoë, honey, get up!"

My eyes shoot open and then slam shut again because my ceiling light is flicking on and off, on and off, on and off, and completely blinding me.

"We're late and I really need your help this morning," my mother says.

I open my eyes to see Mom hopping on one foot while trying to ram her other foot into a perfectly innocent pair of panty hose. "Stop it, Mom!" I jump out of bed and grab the flimsy nylon away from her. "You'll shred them and then it'll look like you've been attacked by piranhas."

She balances herself in the doorway while I coax the nylons slowly up her ankle. "You have to take it up an inch at a time; you **don't shove your leg in whole, like a horse's head going into a feed bag.**"

"I know, I know. You've got much more patience than I do. But what I really need is for you to get Gram's cereal ready for me. I'm putting you in charge so I don't have to worry, okay?"

"Okay."

"Good. Because I've got a very busy day today and I can't be even a second late. Because it's going to be very—"

"I know, I know." I yawn. **"Very busy."**

$\mathcal{O}$nce I am dressed, I hunt for Grandma. Which isn't very hard—I just follow the sound of her tongue clicking against her teeth until I find her in her room, sitting in her flowered chair and looking at a framed picture of me as a little kid. Her face is peaceful, as if she's remembering something nice that I did—like not interrupt her when she told me a story for the millionth time about her mother making her scrub all the floors in the house on her hands and knees, so how come I can't rinse my dishes before putting them in the dishwasher?

She looks up when she sees me. "Hello, little girl," she says. "Would you like some candy?"

I'm not sure why she's calling me little girl, but who's going to argue when there's candy at stake? I hurry over to the candy bowl, which is nearly empty, and take a few butterscotch chews wrapped in gold paper. "Thanks, Grandma. I'm going to go make your breakfast. Do you want Fiber Buds, like Mom says you should have, or can I slip you some of my Froot Loops?"

"What's that?"

"I said, Buds or Loops? Personally, I'd recommend the Loops. You had enough Buds yesterday." I walk toward the kitchen, letting her think about it for a bit, weigh her options. With one, she suffers through short-term gagging but enjoys the comfort of a regular bathroom schedule for the next twenty-four. With the other, **she gets a five-minute slice of heaven, but the trains might not leave the station on time.**

It's a trade-off.

Okay. Bowls ready. Milk and spoon standing by. Cereal boxes open and on counter. I just need her decision. "Grandma?" She doesn't answer, so I run back to her room to make sure she didn't fall asleep and drop the only toddler picture of me before I knocked out my front teeth in an incident involving my Big Wheel and another kid's lousy trike. I never said my toddlerhood was pretty.

"Gram?"

The moment I'm back in her room, she smiles and claps her hands in front of her face. "Would you like to hear about my son, when he was a boy?"

I sit on her bed. **There's not much I like more than hearing stories about my dad when he was little.** "Yeah."

"Lawrence was the handsomest little boy in the neighborhood. Tall for his age, with thick dark curls, just like yours. He had a best friend named Poppy. She was a little girl who lived in the apartment above us. The two of them were together day and night, until it came time for them to start school. On the very first day, Lawrence came home upset. And when I asked him what was wrong, he asked me if Poppy was a girl or a boy."

I giggle. "He didn't know?"

"No. In those days, girls wore their hair shorter." Grandma stopped to stare at a fingernail. Then she points across the room. "Ah. Another hangnail. Would you pass me that nail file on the dresser?"

I jump up and hand it to her. "So what did you tell him?"

Gram looks up from her nail. "I told him she was a girl, of course. And did he carry on! Cried all night."

Poor Dad. "What about Poppy?"

She shook her head. "He never played with her again. Little beasts from school teased him about playing with a girl, so that was the end of it."

"Wow." Just then it hits me. Maybe it's a good thing about the little beasts. Dad could have wound up marrying Poppy instead of Mom, and who knows what might have happened? I might have been born to some other parents. Parents who made me learn to play the harp or feed chickens instead of watching TV. Or, worse, I could have been born a boy.

"Would you get him for me?" Grandma asks.

"Get who?"

"Lawrence. I don't want him to be late for school. He

always sleeps in. Stays up too late watching that detective show. What's it called? *Magnum* . . . something?"

What? "Um, Grandma, Lawrence isn't exactly your little boy anymore. He doesn't live down the hall . . ."

Her eyes flash wicked mad. **"Who are you? And what have you done with my Lawrence?"**

"I'm Zoë . . ."

"Who?"

I sit still for a second, staring at her. Then I just smile a small smile and stand up to go—partly because Grandma's mind is freaking me out. I'm not sure what to say, and I want to get out of there before it happens again.

The other partly is because I want to get Mom out of the house. Fast.

Smartin Granitstein Is Vile. There Are NO Exceptions to This Rule

I'm late for school because I had to stand at Grandma's door and lie to Mom that Gram was getting dressed so Mom wouldn't find out about her thinking Dad's still alive. I got Mom out of the house, but I've missed morning announcements *and* Ingrid Dorfman's oral presentation on the Evolution of the Ballet Slipper. Which I think must have been pretty dull and pretty short, 'cause as far as I know ballet slippers have always looked the same.

I haven't started working on my own oral presentation and Mrs. Patinkin, who clearly considers me the class Welcome Wagon, assigns Maisie as my partner. I don't mind. It'll give me the perfect chance to prevent Maisie from moving over to the dark side. I smile and stare out the window. **Maisie might not know it yet, but she is, in actual fact, one very lucky new kid.**

Maisie pulls a chair up to my desk. "So what's our topic?" Her long black hair is tucked behind her ears, one of which has three silver studs in it.

"What topic?" I ask.

She laughs and taps my forehead with her knuckles. "Of the project. *Duh*."

"I don't have one yet," I explain.

"Oh. When did Mrs. P assign it?"

"Don't call her Mrs. P. She has a thing about that."

"Oh."

"Last Thursday," I say.

Maisie's eyebrows just about hit the ceiling and for one brief moment I wonder if she really *is* mean. Since Thursday my schedule has been very tight, and what kind of kid wouldn't understand that?

"I've been busy," I explain. **Not that the Zoë Lama should have to explain anything** to someone who hasn't even been at school long enough to have a reputation. "Extraordinarily busy. But it doesn't matter. I work fast."

"Okay," says Maisie. "Well, I think we should do motorcycles, then. Or maybe cigarettes."

Motorcycles? Cigarettes? **For a passing moment I actually doubt I can save the girl.** "No. I'm not a fan. Of either."

"Okay, how about balloons? I once read—"

"NO!" I shout. Maisie's elbow slips off my desk and I grab her arm to keep her upright. "I mean, balloons are really for babies, don't you think? I was thinking of something more sophisticated. Like . . ." For some reason Grandma's face pops into my mind. "Like gray hair."

Her mouth sneers up, all the way to her nose. "Gray hair? Gross."

Sneering might not qualify as mean, but I have to say, **this attitude isn't pretty.**

"It's perfect," I say. "Why Hair Goes Gray. And I'm pretty sure I can pluck a few actual gray hairs when my grandma's sleeping. Then we can have a live sample. Or dead. My grandma's not dead. Not yet. Just her hair is. Everybody's hair is."

Maisie looks a little gray herself. "Whatever."

While she's writing *Gray Hair* at the top of her notepad, I decide that's a pretty agreeable thing to do. **It's time to get to work on saving her.** "So, are you enjoying the school so far?"

She shrugs and bites off the tip of a carrot that she, apparently, keeps in her pants pocket. "S'okay. Nobody talked to me all day yesterday, though. Nobody but some girls at the side of the school. Older girls."

Here it is. My moment. "If you don't mind a little friendly advice, **it's probably better if you stick to girls your own age.**"

She just blinks at me and chews. Then blinks and chews some more.

"What I mean is . . ." I pause, but only because a note launch has come in from the northeast, hitting me in the right temple. "Excuse me," I say, before unscrunching the note, which is from Susannah. I look up to see her peering at me from behind her glasses and smiling, so I give her the secret wave. Which is too secret to reveal.

The note says,

> Dear Zoë,
>   I can see you're busy with a customer. I just thought I'd remind you of one thing. Some people are just plain mean. Born mean and die mean. And no amount of meddling can change it.
>   Signed,
>   A Concerned Friend
>   P.S. I don't think Smartin owns a toothbrush. He leered at me while he was taking his coat off and his teeth were covered in fur.

I crumple the note and stuff it into my pocket. Then, ever so casually, I turn to face Smartin. He glances over at me and winks. Slowly, his mouth spreads into a big, wide, creepy grin. **Sure enough, his teeth are as fuzzy as a lamb.**

"Vile!" I say, turning away from the horror.

"That's not what the *ladies* tell me," Smartin says.

Then, the most unbelievable thing happens. Maisie nudges my arm and whispers, "He's cute."

Smartin Granitstein? Cute? In the entire history of Allencroft Middle School, not one single female has ever, ever had such an outrageous thought pass through her head. I can personally, completely, 100 percent promise it, and if anyone can prove to me that they have had such a monstrous thought, I'll hand over my *Garage Girls* Season One DVD. No. I'll hand over Season One *and* Season Two.

"Maisie," I say, moving closer to her. The situation is so-o-o much more serious than I previously thought. I pat her on the back and smile. "You seem like a nice kid, so I'm gonna help you out. In every school there are certain . . . Unwritten Rules that newcomers might not pick up on right away. And how could you possibly know them? You couldn't. So, here's what I'm going to do. I'm going to personally guide you through this transition period and make sure you end up with all the right people. We'll start immediately. **Unwritten Rule Number Three is—**

Smartin Granitstein is vile. There are *no* exceptions to Unwritten Rule Number Three."

This is the part when Maisie will be astonished. And it's entirely possible she will cry a few tears of gratitude and relief. She'll be overwhelmed by my offer—which is unusual. Typically, people approach *me* for advice. It's rare that I extend complete life guidance to someone who's been recently expelled from school, let alone stripped of good standing.

"Why?" she asks. "Why is it so important to you that I don't end up with the wrong people? And how do *you* know who the wrong people are, anyway?"

No one has ever questioned my advice before. It's Unwritten Rule #2.

"Maisie." I try again. "Look around you. There are . . . what? Twelve or thirteen other boys in the room, every one of them more appealing than Fartin' Smartin."

Maisie looks concerned for the first time. "You mean…?"

"Yes! I would not steer you wrong." I point toward the window side of the classroom. "Now here we have a row of three or four tolerable specimens. They have clean hair, at least one of them is wearing a matching set of shoes, and **I'll bet none of them has ever strained milk** through his gym sock to see if it would taste like apple-cider vinegar."

She looks around the classroom, resting her eyes on the young men. "You think it?"

"I know it."

She stuffs the stubby end of the carrot back into her pocket and crosses her arms. "So, do you give out copies of this rule book?"

"Absolutely not. A rule book full of unwritten rules can only exist inside my mind. Because the rules are *unwritten*."

"So . . . the rules are invisible," Maisie says.

I sigh. "You could say that."

"Maybe you should call them Invisible Rules. It sounds better."

"I *prefer* unwritten."

Maisie considers this for a moment, then nods. "Right. So what's Unwritten Rule Number Two?"

Aahh, how I love it when they're ready to learn!

Keep Your Friends Close and Your Clients Closer

"How's your grandma? I miss her candy dish," Susannah says on the way to Mr. Lindsay's Winter Dance Committee meeting in the library. We were told we could bring our lunches because Mrs. Kettleby trusts that we're old enough now not to spill soup on the library carpet. I've got my lunch bag and pen and paper in one hand and my new client in the other. I'd like to keep Maisie close, where I can keep an eye on her, at least until she's fully trained.

"Grandma and her candy dish are great," I say. It's not a total lie. **The candy dish is doing very well. Grandma, on the other hand, not so much.** I wish it was the other way around.

Laurel squeezes my arm. "Tell Gram we're coming to visit soon, and I have a thing for jelly beans these days."

In a few short days the girls are coming over to watch a once-in-a-lifetime TV show. *The Garage Girls Behind-the-Scenes Sneak Peek.* "I'll tell her," I say, thanking the heavens for Grandma's doctor appointments.

It's hard not to vomit once we get in the library, because the last person you'd ever think you'd see in the library is in the library. Sitting at the Winter Dance Committee planning table right beside Mr. Lindsay. It's Smartin—with both ends of his straw up his nostrils, like a ring in a bull's nose.

I squeeze Maisie's arm tighter and guide her to the chair farthest away from Smartin. Maisie giggles when she sees him, forcing me to shake my head at her and whisper, "Be strong," before I shoot him a look that says, *Stay away!*

"Welcome, girls and guys," says Mr. Lindsay, who is looking seriously handsome as he stands up and rubs his hands together so hard I almost expect to see sparks fly. Hopefully not onto Smartin's oily hair, or there might be a grease fire. Mr. Lindsay plops his notebook down between two LameWizards who haven't once looked up from their electronic battles. "I'm going to get myself a coffee," Handsome Mr. Lindsay says. "So you kids might as well start eating your lunch and maybe jot down any ideas you might have for the dance." He smiles and gives us a wink. "Back in a second." And he's gone.

"Mr. Lindsay's very handsome, don't you think?" I say as I watch him jog down the hall.

Susannah and Laurel sigh and nod.

Smartin snorts. And I'm quite certain he means to snort. "If you enjoy guys like that."

Susannah says, "Guys like what, Smartin? With proper hygiene?"

"What's hygiene again?" asks Laurel, who, sadly, has given up on her quest for color and has once again returned to wearing head-to-toe blue.

"Cleanliness," says Maisie. I'm so proud of her I could burst.

Smartin says, "Cleanliness is for dorks." He pushes about a shovelful of pasta into his mouth and chews with noodles slopping out onto his chin.

I say, "Cleanliness is for boyfriends. Something you'll *never* be."

Smartin smiles at me. There's green stuff in his teeth. "Let's make out."

"Ugh!"

"It's time you and me go public with our love."

"You wish." I spin my chair around so I can no longer see his wormy chin.

"Let's play a game," Susannah says, taking a bite of her

tuna sandwich. "We'll take turns confessing the meanest thing we've done in the last month. Maisie, you can go first." I know what she's doing here. She's testing Maisie. To see how truly mean she is. Or isn't.

Maisie sips from her thermos and says, "Um . . . I don't know. **I accidentally killed a spider by running over it with my bicycle tire. Is that mean?**"

Susannah laughs. "C'mon, you can do better than that. I'll show you how to play." She adjusts her dark glasses and looks up at the ceiling. "Okay. **Last week I swapped my Gummi Bears with Laurel's blue ones** at a sleepover, in the dark, and Laurel ate them, saying they were the best blue gummies she'd ever tasted."

Laurel chokes on her creamy blue soup (her mother must go through buckets of food coloring). "Hey! That's nasty!"

"It seems nasty at first," Susannah explains. "But I just thought you'd see that they all taste good. Not just the blue ones. And I was right."

Slowly, Laurel's face relaxes. "They actually *were* pretty good," she says. **"Okay, I'll go next.** Last week when my sister scammed my new turtleneck behind my back and slobbered mustard all over it, I took her toothbrush . . ." She stops and bites her bottom lip.

"**Yeah?**" Susannah, Maisie, and I all say at once.

Laurel sits back and shakes her head. "No. I shouldn't say. It's *really* bad."

"Say!" I blurt out.

"Okay, but remember, I saved up for six weeks to buy that turtleneck." She looks each one of us in the eye before saying it. "**I rubbed Victoria's toothbrush in the toilet.**"

"Awgh!" We all slump with the gross-osity of it.

"Wait," I say. "Did you rub it *on* the toilet, or *in* it?"

Laurel tries not to smile. "In it."

"Total toilet-water penetration?" Susannah asks.

"**Full dunkage.**"

"Whoa," Susannah says, leaning back in her chair. She's gotten herself new dark glasses, I notice for the first time. These ones are huge and very round. They make her look like a supermagnified fly. "So far, you win. Who's next?"

"Forget this game," I say, hoping to change the topic before it's Maisie's turn again. Besides, I need to have some brilliant dance ideas before Handsome Mr. Lindsay gets back, or **he'll think I'm an idiot and won't want to meet my mother and apply for the open position of husband.** "Everyone close your eyes for thirty seconds and imagine the most perfect dance ever and what it would be like. Then, when I say time's up, write down three key elements."

Laurel looks worried. "My mother won't let me go unless there's one chaperone for every five kids. She's worried I'll get French-kissed."

Smartin looks up from licking the inside of his lunch bag clean and laughs. "You? French-kissed?"

"It's possible, Smartin!" I snap. **"I'm sure there are many boys in this school who find Laurel overwhelmingly French-kissable.** Aren't there, Susannah?"

"Hundreds. Maybe more," Susannah says. Despite the squabbles, we three are still a team.

"Thanks, guys." Laurel punches me in the shoulder. Susannah she punches, too, but a bit harder because of the gummies. "You're the best."

I smile. "I said nothing that isn't true. Now get to work, everybody. Three things you'd like to see."

What would make it perfect for me would be being dropped off by my mother's new husband. My stepdad.

Especially a stepdad who looks like Handsome Mr. Lindsay.
I write,

The Three Things That Make
Handsome Mr. Lindsay Perfect

1. He likes kids so much he's even nice to Smartin. No small achievement, if you ask me. Plus, he's got those math tools in his shirt pocket. I'll bet the circle drawing thingy could have gotten the eraser out of my nose when I was three.
2. There's not a speck of fur on his teeth. I checked while he was bossing us around.
3. That hand rubbing, though some-times annoying, could probably get the circulation back in a frostbitten foot.

Handsome Mr. Lindsay flies back into the room, plops his coffee cup onto the round table, and rubs his hands again. "All righty. Let's see what you've all come up with."

Everyone reads their lists. **Smartin wants an electric bull.** Which is idiotic, but Handsome Mr. Lindsay pretends it's not the lamest answer in the world and asks Maisie what she's come up with. She says she likes streamers, especially when they're twisted, and could the punch please not be red, because **she saw the movie** *Carrie* **and gets freaked out by red liquids at school dances.**

I couldn't care less about the color of the punch. I'm just happy she doesn't say balloons. **This kid can't possibly be mean if she decorates with streamers.**

Susannah wants to have queen and king elections. She says it'll give the dance some real class. Everyone knows she's planning to be the queen, since she's the most famous. Sort of.

When he gets to me, I slip my paper into my pocket and explain that I was too busy managing everyone else to dream up any good dance stuff of my own. Handsome Mr. Lindsay gets this weird grin on his face and says, "Zoë, you'd make a great chairwoman of the dance committee, since you won't hesitate to throw your weight around to keep everybody in line." Since I weigh about as much as a wiener dog, everyone laughs. But I know he really means I'll get results.

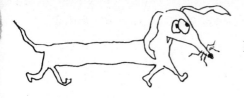

"If it's all the same to you, I prefer chairgirl," I say.

Handsome Mr. Lindsay laughs. "Then chairgirl it is."

I assign people their duties; Maisie gets "decorations" because of the streamers, Susannah gets "theme" because she owns a tiara, Laurel gets "food" because she'll need some color control, the LameWizards get "ticket sales," and Smartin gets "music" because Mr. Lindsay insisted he be included. I, of course, will have my hands full making sure they do everything deliciously perfect. Handsome Mr. Lindsay agrees with all my decisions.

All his agreeableness needs to be added to my list, so I pull out my paper and hide it under the table. I cross out the title and change it to say, **The *Four* Things that Make Handsome Mr. Lindsay Perfect.**

"Wait, Mr. Lindsay," says Maisie. **"What about a name for the dance?"**

"Ah! Good point. Any ideas?"

Susannah sits up tall. **"Moonlight Delight!"**

"Snowball City," says Smartin.

"Snow Snow Snow," Maisie says.

What are these people thinking? **"The Wondrous Winter Ball,"** I suggest.

"**Magic at Midnight,**" says a Lame Wizard. Personally, I doubt he'll be having any midnight magic. He'll be tucked under his *Lord of the Rings* comforter, wearing headgear.

"Magic at Midnight?" squeaks Susannah. "The dance ends at nine!"

"Good ideas, folks!" says Handsome Mr. Lindsay. "But I'm sort of leaning toward Martin's name. Why don't we just call it the Snow Ball?"

"Yes!" shouts Smartin, clenching his dirty hand into a fist and punching the air.

So that's how our dance gets the worst name possible for a winter dance. The Snow Ball.

I can see the food fight already.

Sometimes Death by Puckered Parrot Is Worth the Risk

"She flinched," Susannah says as we step onto the elevator.

She and Laurel are coming over to watch *The Garage Girls Behind-the-Scenes Sneak Peek.* **For three weeks,** ever since it was first advertised on TV, **we've been planning this.** Mom is taking Grandma for her annual physical and won't be home till after dinner, so we are going to watch it at my house. We pooled our allowances on the way home and bought **two chocolate bars, a bag of ketchup chips, nine Gummi Sharks, and a bottle of 7-Up, the most easy-to-dye-blue soda we could find.**

All three Garage Girls are going to be interviewed in their very own houses. We'll get to see their real-life boyfriends, best friends, even their dogs. I could barely sleep last night, I was so excited. Devon,

the tall skinny one with the long black hair, is supposed to have a bed that hangs from the ceiling
by chains.

"Who flinched?" Laurel asks Susannah.

"Maisie," says Susannah. "Did you see her
when I asked her about the meanest thing she'd
done? Did you see how freaked out she got?"

Laurel and I race to push the number eight button and then stare at Susannah, who is clearly beginning to
lose her mind. "No," we both say.

"Oh, come on," Susannah moans. "Her eyes darted
around and she got all fidgety."

"She was opening her lunch bag," I say.

"She knows I'm onto her." Susannah, as usual, starts
pushing on the door-open button about three floors too
early. Laurel and I should really thank whoever designed the
doors to refuse to open between floors. Because you truly
cannot trust people to *not* do moronic things like that.

"Maybe she forgot about that whole summer and rec-
ognizes you from TV," Laurel says. Then she grins. "Maybe
she wants your autograph."

Susannah fake-laughs. "Ha ha."

Laurel shoulder-bumps Susannah. "Come on! Love ya

like my number two." **I love it when my BFISs share the love. It's good for business.**

Susannah smiles. A bit. "All right. Number two right back at ya."

Okay. Enough love. The elevator doors heave themselves open and we step into the hall. "I've been watching for signs of meanness," I say. "The kid's clean. It's possible that Nicholas really did write that note. Maisie might not have known what she was handing you and simply went on an innocent canoe ride with Nicholas."

Susannah looks shocked. "But that would mean I got dumped. **I can't have been dumped.** I've got a reputation for never having been dumped and I plan on keeping it squeaky-clean until I die. Maybe even longer. It's very important to me."

Okay. Time to change the subject. "You know what else I heard about Devon from *The Garage Girls*? I heard she has a tiger pit in her backyard with seven white tigers." We stop in front of my apartment. I turn the key in the lock and poke my head inside before we go in—just to be sure no one's on the couch watching *Jeopardy!* because her physical got canceled or something.

Laurel shouts, "That's animal cruelty! What tiger wants

to sit around watching Devon sunbathing and drinking champagne coolies all day?"

We plop ourselves on the couch and lay out all the treats. And while Laurel drops blue food coloring into the soda, I divvy up the candy. Only I give all the chocolate to Susannah, who is clearly worried about Maisie's possible truthfulness.

Suddenly Susannah brightens up. Chocolate can do that. "Oh! **I have *major* news and it's about you, Zoë.**"

Major news is always delicious, but especially delicious when it's about me. I drop my candy and slide closer. "What?"

Susannah scrunches up her nose and bites her bottom lip. **"It's about a certain boy who wants to ask a certain girl a certain question."** Then she sits back, confident that everyone gets what she means. Which we so don't.

Laurel takes a huge sip of blue pop and says, "Huh?"

I ask, "Would you mind translating? And this time, could you please leave out the word *certain*?"

Susannah's head rolls a bit, which really means she's rolling her eyes behind her sunglasses. "Riley is planning to ask you to the dance."

"Really?" I hug my knees and smile like crazy.

"Yes," she says. "But he doesn't want to ask like any other boy would. He wants it to be special. I heard from a certain source—"

"Hey," I warn. I thought I'd been very clear about the word *certain*.

"Sorry," she says. "I heard he's going to get down on one knee in the cafeteria. And that he's going to do it on hamburger-and-french-fry day so he can share his fries!"

Outrageous. **I love fries.** Riley's pretty good, too.

Then Laurel picks up the remote and points it at the TV. "How do you work this thing, anyway?"

I grab it and turn on the set. But no show comes on, only fuzzy gray stuff and fuzzy gray sounds. I try to turn the channel, but every single channel has the same picture: nothing but electric lint.

"It's broken?" wails Laurel. "The *Sneak Peek* starts in exactly seven minutes!"

"We can't even get to *my* house in that time," Susannah says.

"Hang on." I turn the set off, then on again. Same gray fuzz. **This is bad. Very, very bad.** I run into the kitchen and call my mom on her cell phone.

"Jocelyn Costello here," she says in her office voice, even though she's in the car. I can hear Grandma singing along to Harry Connick Jr. in the background.

"Mom. Emergency!" I say. "It's six and a half minutes till *Garage Girls Behind-the-Scenes Sneak Peek* and the TV isn't working! What button do I press to get the picture back?"

I really don't like what she says next. "Uh-oh."

"What? Uh-oh?"

All I hear is Grandma blowing her nose.

"Mom, we're down to five and a half minutes."

"Honey, you know how crazy it's been . . . and that sometimes I forget to do things because I have to juggle a busy career, a boisterous daughter, an aging parent, and a household full of bills . . ."

"Mom, no! Please say it's not like that time you forgot to pay the phone bill!"

"I'm sorry, honey. I meant to pay the cable, I really did. But I remember now—Grandma slipped and got jammed between the toilet and the tub. Remember we had to ask Mr. Flotsam next door to help?"

I remember. I remember. But this should not prevent three girls from missing out on the most important television event of the twenty-first century! I glance over at Laurel and Susannah, who are eating their candy like there isn't a worry in the world. **How can I do this to them, my number one and number two BFIS?** And with Susannah in a delicate mental state?

I can't.

"What did she say to do?" Laurel asks. Blue Gummi shark fins are stuck between her teeth.

I stand up and run to the door. "I'll be right back!"

As hard as I can, I pound on Mr. Flotsam's door. "Mr. Flotsam! Emergency! It's Zoë from next door!"

From inside, he shouts, "Just soak her hips in olive oil and pull her forward."

"No! It's not that. Do you have a TV?"

"I told your granny I'm not going to snuggle with her anymore during _Jeopardy!_ She shouts out all the answers."

"No, I need the TV!" There's nothing but silence. "Mr. Flotsam? Are you there?"

The _Jeopardy!_ music blares through the door.

Susannah and Laurel's heads poke out from my apartment. "Zoë, come back. It's starting in three minutes!"

I race to the next door. Miss Carnegie hates me, but she's

got cable. Not only that, she's got high-definition. I pound until my hands ache and yell into the door, "Miss Carnegie! It's Zoë from down the hall! I need to borrow a TV."

"It'll be a cold day in Tahiti before I lend you neighbors anything EVER AGAIN!" she says.

"But we've never borrowed—"

"That Flotsam character next door borrowed my hair dryer in 1999, and he still hasn't given it back. I don't know why—he didn't have any hair then and he doesn't have any now!"

"But we don't actually need to remove your TV . . ."

"And Clara What's-her-name borrowed two plums in July of 2004. Do you think she's repaid me? **Come around in fifteen years,** I'll probably still be waiting!"

Actually, I don't think I will come around anytime soon or in fifteen years. She's too cranky.

The next door is Mrs. Grungen's. And **I don't know what she does in there, but the whole hallway stinks from it.** I slow down and knock lightly. "Mrs. Grungen, are you in there?" I'm not really sure I want to know the answer.

"Eh?"

"It's Zoë Costello from down the hall. I need to ask a favor."

I can hear her walker clop, clop, clopping toward me. Then the door bursts open and gets choked by the chain. One of her horrible yellowish bloodshot eyes peers out at me. "What is it?" **When she talks, the prickly hairs on her chin scratch against the door frame.**

I blurt out, **"Well, you see, the cable went out** and it's about thirty seconds till *The Garage Girls Behind-the-Scenes Sneak Peek* and my two best friends in the school are over and **we'd do anything if you'd just let us watch your TV** for just half an hour."

She goes silent. A floorboard squeaks.

"Anything?" she asks.

I wipe a spray of spittle off my cheek, forcing my brain not to think about what microbes might lurk in the saliva of a lady who smells like Mrs. Grungen. "Anything," I say.

The door slams shut, then a chain rattles and it creaks open all the way. Finally I can see what is causing all that stench.

Right in the middle of the room is a giant parrot in a cage bigger than a fridge. And I'm not sure if he's dead or alive, because half his feathers are gone and the skin where the feathers should be is all puckered and pasty. Eventually he coughs, which suggests that he's alive, but the cough is so rattly and deep it makes me wonder for how long.

After this, there's some good news and some bad news. The good news is that within twenty seconds we're watching *The Garage Girls Behind-the-Scenes Sneak Peek*. Alexandra, Devon, and Lucia are right now lying in the sun beside Lucia's pool and a butler is serving them icy pink drinks and brownies. It looks like The Life, I'll say that much.

The bad news is that **the "anything" I agreed to is rubbing Mrs. Grungen's foot lotion onto Pavel the parrot's puckered and pasty skin parts.** The lotion smells like moldy onions and feels like chunky peanut butter and is stuck under my fingernails, and every time I reach into Pavel's cage I have to hold my breath or risk permanent lung damage from barely alive parrot stink.

I gotta get my mom that assistant. Quick.

Sixty Seconds of Happy Kicks Jeopardy!'s Butt

"That's why I put Laurel in charge of food for the dance," I explain to my mother, who is lying in a bath full of bubbles for her nightly "half-hour slice of heaven." She's got candles lit by her feet, a pile of fashion magazines by her head, and a big glass of wine in her hand. **It's supposed to be her "*me* time," but I haven't seen her all day, so she changed it to "*we* time." Just for tonight.** "I knew Laurel would follow directions and I want the food to be perfect," I say. "I want every single student at Allencroft to be happy with my selections."

Mom looks at me and blinks a few times. "Don't you mean Laurel's selections?"

I laugh. "Yeah, right! We'd have all the blue food groups and nothing else. I've recommended we be globally conscious in every choice."

"Globally conscious?"

"Yup. Every choice needs to fit within our special-needs specifications."

She flips through her magazine. "Which are?"

"Lactose-free, diabetic, gluten-free, low-sodium, low-cholesterol—which, luckily, falls under the same guidelines **as low-fat, Muslim, Hindu, kosher, vegetarian, and bland."**

She looks up from her magazine. "Bland? Isn't that a bad thing?"

I know this one by heart. "No—bland is a category of foods that contain a low element of fat and fiber in order to ensure proper gastrointestinal balance."

"Well. Very impressive. Sounds like you're a terrific chairwoman."

"I prefer chairgirl."

Mom squirts a little more bubble bath into the tub and swishes it around. Then she hands me her magazines, leans back, and folds a washcloth across her eyes. "Do you mind, honey? I just need five minutes to meditate."

"Whatever." I stand up and start to leave, accidentally dropping the magazines onto the bathroom floor.

"Be careful with those. There are some papers from Grandma's doctor in there."

"I'm careful, I'm careful." As I gather them into a pile, I sweep a thick brochure onto the top. But the model on the cover is no supermodel. **She's older than Grandma and she's smiling like crazy at a nurse who is feeding her soup.** And the nurse looks like she's having the best time she's ever had in her nursey life. She's smiling so big, her bottom teeth are showing.

Across the top it says Shady Gardens Home for Seniors. What?

Quickly, I open the brochure to see pictures of old people sitting in dumpy beige flowery bedrooms, and old people sitting on dumpy brown flowery sofas, and old people leaning their heads together and **smiling for the camera, like they're so happy their families stuck them in this beige-and-brown flowery prison of dumpiness.** What I want to know is what kind of flowers come in beige and brown anyway?

"Mom," I finally say.

"Mm?"

"Where did you get this?" I lift the washcloth off her eyes and hold out the brochure.

She opens her eyes, looks at it, and sighs. "Oh. You saw it."

"Uh, yeah."

"Grandma's doctor gave it to me. He said her Alzheimer's is getting worse and that **it's time we start looking at our options."**

There's that word again. "Options like nursing homes?"

She nods. "I'm afraid so, sweetie."

"Then look at other options, too. Like me staying home from school. **I'll quit and look after Grandma full-time."**

Mom just looks at me. "That's *not* one of our options. Her doctor recommended a full-care facility."

"Then maybe a special nurse can come live with us and take care of her. That would work. We could give the nurse my bedroom—"

Mom laughs sadly. "That's far too expensive, and I don't think you would like bunking with me. I snore."

"Then what about getting her another doctor? For all we know, Grandma's doctor might have been the *worst* student in medical school. Somebody's got to graduate at the bottom of the class, right?"

"Zoë . . ."

"Everyone always assumes every doctor is a genius, but there has to be one who was the idiot of all the geniuses. There *has* to be! Do we really know for sure it's not him?"

"Dr. Milner is not an idiot."

"I didn't say that. I said the idiot genius."

"Zoë, I'm very tired. Please go finish your homework."

"Only if you promise to look into Dr. Milner's medical school records."

"Zoë!" She pushes hair out of her face and reaches for a towel. "Homework. Now."

*B*ack in my room, I lie on my bed and try to forget about Shady Gardens. Surrounded in pencil crayons, **I'm drawing a picture of how I would look if I were tall.** I draw my legs super long with gorgeous red boots and I draw a striped miniskirt instead of my usual plain old denim skirt, because I once saw a fashion model wearing a blue-and-white-striped miniskirt and, wow, did she look cool.

Grandma swishes in carrying a cup of steaming cocoa with whipped cream and sets it on my night-stand. "Hello, dear. I thought you'd like a nice hot drink."

"I would!" I sit up on my knees and sip it as Grandma examines my drawing. It's like having the old Grandma back. The one who knows when you need cocoa before you even know it yourself and she doesn't glare at you when you drink it while kneeling on your bed.

It makes this cocoa taste better than any she's ever made.

"This is a fine self-portrait. And the skirt looks French. **Very chic, Zoë.** I like the shading on the boots."

Another awesome thing about Grandma. **She knows a good self-portrait when she sees one,** even when the legs are drawn wishfully long. She does *not* deserve to be jumbo-smiled at by that Shady Gardens nurse, who really needs to get herself something better to smile about.

"Thanks. I learned the shading part at school."

"Your teacher should give you an A." Grandma snaps her teeth and sits down on the bed. "Did I tell you my Lawrence won the regional swim meet?"

She's told me hundreds of times, but I *love* this story. "No, Gram. Tell me now."

"It was just last week."

"Last week?" I ask, hoping she'll correct herself. **I really, really don't want her thinking Dad's alive again.** It's proof positive that she's getting worse. He won that swim meet about a zillion years ago, when he was not much older than me!

She looks at me like I'm dense and waves a hand toward the window. I notice now her hand is shaking. "Yes. Last week. At the rec center. The pool there is nearly Olympic size."

Okay, I don't know what to do. Stop her and tell her that her son, my dad, is not only grown up, but actually no longer alive? **Would she even believe me if I corrected her?** Maybe I should just shut up and leave her to her happy memories. I put my cocoa down. My stomach doesn't feel so good.

The trouble is, and it's very selfish trouble, I love to hear about him. I could listen to these stories all day, because it helps me build memories of him.

Besides, it'll give her a minute of something to think about besides Fiber Buds and *Jeopardy!* Wouldn't sixty seconds of happy kick-butt over a whole season of *Jeopardy!*?

"Oh yeah," I say. "The swim meet last week. What happened again?"

Her hands settle down and her face relaxes. Her eyes get all dreamy. "My Lawrence was so fast, from the moment the starting pistol fired, he was in the lead. He swam four lengths in freestyle and thought the race was over. He stopped and pulled off his cap before the photographers zoomed in for their victory shots. Well, the crowd went wild, because there were two more lengths to complete. The other swimmers were catching up and Lawrence was still fixing his hair. Finally, as his competitors somersaulted against the end and pushed on for the final two lengths, Lawrence realized his mistake and took off again. And do you know, he still won that race?"

"Wow."

"They said he had time to eat an entire banana split while he waited for the others to catch up. But still, he won." She shakes her head and wipes a tear from her eye. "Without so much as a bathing cap. He left it on the pool deck, at the photographers' feet."

"Wicked," I say. "I'll have to congratulate him when he gets home."

She looks confused. **"But he _is_ home. He's in the bathroom right now."**

"No, that's Mom. And she'll be out any minute. So let's just get you down the hall to your room before she gets out." _And hears our conversation,_ I don't say.

Grandma stands up and shuffles toward the door. "I'm quite certain it's Lawrence. I'll just knock."

"No!" I jump up and grab her arm. If Mom knows Grandma is talking crazy, it'll only send her running to

Shady Gardens to book a room with a view. "I think it's much better if we get you straight to bed." Gently I guide her down the hall toward her room, praying she doesn't call for him—

"Lawrence?" she calls as we approach the bathroom door. "Lawrence?"

"Shh! Quiet, Gram, please!"

"I just need to tell him about his college application forms," Grandma says, stopping right beside the bathroom. Before I can stop her, she knocks. "Lawrence?"

I hold my breath, waiting for Mom to fling open the door and Grandma to call Lawrence, and Mom to give me a look that says, *It's time, Zoë.* Then I hear it.

The blow dryer. Mom's drying her hair. She hasn't heard a thing!

Grandma says, "I've heard that Harvard has a very good business school. **I want to tell him to apply to Harvard** first."

Oh boy. I pull her forward. "I'll tell him when he gets out of the bathroom. But let's hurry up. We've got to get you into your room quick!" She takes one step, then stops and turns back toward the bathroom, looking upset.

The blow dryer stops and I hear Mom humming. I've got about thirty seconds before she opens the door.

"Come on, Gram! Let's go. Please!"

Finally, Grandma turns to follow me. "I was just thinking," she says as we walk. "A nice hot cup of cocoa sounds good. **Can you go get my granddaughter?** She'll make it the way I like it."

I sigh, guiding her into her bed and flicking off the light. Then I kiss her forehead and pull the sheets up under her chin. "Close your eyes, Grandma. I'll go tell her."

"Her name's Zoë. She makes wonderful cocoa."

I smile what really doesn't feel like a smile and close the door.

Never Lift for Yourself What a Fifth-Grader Is Willing to Lift for You

I hate trumpets. Not a Tuesday or a Thursday goes by without me wishing desperately that I'd fought harder for a flute in music class. Flutes are so pretty, and Laurel's fingers look so delicate pressing its beautiful silver keys. But the best part is that you get to hold your mouth in a little kissy shape while you play.

And it doesn't hurt if you're looking at Riley in the clarinet section.

This doesn't work with trumpets. First of all, you have to squeeze the keys hard because these school trumpets are more than a little banged up. Second, **no delicate little kissy-shaped mouth is gonna make any kind of sound from a trumpet.**

The only way I can describe it is, if Avery Buckner was coming at you for a kiss, with his eyes closed romantically behind his smeary glasses, big cracked lips flapping, and the only way you could possibly push him away was with your mouth, you'd scrunch up your lips pretty hard, right? You'd push them as far out as you could, to keep his grimy glasses from touching your nose, and you'd suck in a deep breath all the way down from your toes and blow so hard you'd lose all feeling in your lips.

That's how you blow into a trumpet. It doesn't say that in the music book, but it should.

And I haven't even mentioned the worst part. **It's impossible to see Riley while you're playing because of the big old horn-shaped end.**

Mrs. Day claps her hands and yells that we better redo "Ode to Joy" or our parents will complain after the winter concert. We hold our instruments all ready, and as soon as her stick starts thrashing around, we play like crazy.

My lips are tingling so bad it feels like my mouthpiece is full of miniature bees. I'm not sure I can take it anymore and glance at Sylvia Smye beside me. She isn't doing much better. Her face is nearly purple from blowing and her eyes shoot around wildly. But believe me, every single one of us knows exactly what will happen if we stop playing for any reason.

Instant, nonnegotiable, ego-busting trip directly to the office. Do not pass Go. Do not collect $200.

In the middle of the song, Sylvia folds. The bees got to her. She drops her trumpet to her side and puts up her hand.

Mrs. Day swings her stick sideways, which means everyone better stop their lousy playing—and fast. She asks, "What is it, Sylvia?"

"My lips are tingling real bad this time. And my cheeks hurt. **I think I'm allergic to my trumpet."**

"You can't be allergic to a trumpet. And don't interrupt while we're playing. If you have a problem, kindly enlighten us at the end of the piece. And a, four, three, two, and . . ." She flails the stick around and we start to play again.

This time, when Sylvia sucks in a big breath to begin the next bar, she drops her instrument again in a choking, sputtering fit.

"Sylvia Smye!" Mrs. Day calls. "What did I tell you?"

Between coughs, Sylvia whispers, "I can't help it! I'm drowning in spit from Harrison"—cough—"Huxtable"—cough.

"Nonsense. **How could you possibly know whose saliva you've inhaled?"**

"Because it tastes like his cherry cough drops. I might be catching his cold, I feel like fainting."

Sensing a golden opportunity to rest my buzzing lips, which feel like they might explode, I shoot my hand up into the air. "Excuse me, Mrs. Day. You know it's not like me to interfere in other people's business, but I feel I must inform you that I have actually heard of a case of a severe trumpet allergy."

Mrs. Day's eyes narrow. **With straight dark hair falling down both sides of her face, she looks like someone's closing the curtains on her.** At any moment all we'll see is a nose. "Oh?"

"Yes. It was two years ago, in a middle school just like this. A student complained to her music teacher, who ignored her symptoms. This teacher, too, had never heard of a trumpet allergy. But mouthpieces are made of silver, and skin can react to the nickel content in some silver mouthpieces. The girl's parents sued the school. *Langstaff Middle School v. Alexandria Chutney.*"

Mrs. Day frowns. "Hmm. And what was the outcome of the court case?"

"In the end, things turned out

fine. Alexandria bought herself a gold-plated mouthpiece and her former teacher *eventually* found another job. In a poultry factory in a neighboring town."

As Mrs. Day sucks in a sharp breath, her nostrils flare, and the dark curtains part to show a very pale face. She points her baton at the door. "Take Sylvia to the school nurse right this minute."

Worked like spit!

$\mathcal{W}$ith Sylvia happily stashed away on the nurse's cot, I beat it out of her office and nearly bump into Maisie, who is putting her name on a sign-up sheet for the track team.

"Hey, Maisie," I say. My lips are still buzzing from my trumpet, so I'd like to put off returning to music class as long as I can. "Going out for track?"

She turns around. "Yeah. I love running. I want to run in the Olympics one day. It's been my dream since I was, like, two. Why don't you join, too?"

"Nah. Running's not my thing." I sit down on Principal Renzetti's bench and try to stretch out my lips.

"Oh, please," she begs, sliding onto the bench. "Then I'd have a best friend on the team. It would be so fun."

Whoa. "Did you say . . . best friend?"

"Of course. You're my friend, and if you joined, we'd be together nearly all the time, so you could be my best friend."

Clearly, Maisie has been operating under a misapprehension. Which means she's dangerously confused. Susannah is my number one BFIS, Laurel is my number two. **And everyone knows there's no such thing as a number three BFIS. It's Unwritten Rule #9.** Everyone knows that. It would cheapen the status of number one and number two BFIS.

But how do I tell her?

Maisie smiles at me. I don't want to hurt her feelings. **The poor girl doesn't even realize that it's too early in her training for her to make her own decisions** about things as important as best friends.

Especially best friends like me.

"Maisie," I begin, very gently, "this crazy world we live in is full of rules. And while some rules, like no gum chewing in the halls, may seem lame and even cruel, other rules exist to keep some kind of order in our lives."

She thinks about this, then her eyes light up and she says, "Oh, I get it. Like coming to school at eight forty-five?"

"No. That one is lame and cruel. I was thinking of different rules. Remember the Unwritten Rules?"

"The invisible ones? Sure, I remember." She sits up tall, sets her hands on her lap, and recites, **"Unwritten Rule Number Five—Never Lift for Yourself What a Fifth-Grader Is Willing to Lift for You."**

"Good girl. That's right. They're younger and more limber."

Maisie stares straight ahead, then nods her head. She looks down to scribble something in her notepad.

I continue. **"These Unwritten Rules create a map for us to follow, so we get through our school years with the tiniest amount of stress.** Which brings us to Unwritten Rule Number Nine. See, Maisie, a girl should have a best friend in the school. She can even have two best friends in the school, but only as long as these friends never, ever confuse their status. Otherwise we have chaos. And chaos is not good. See what I'm saying?"

"Sure. Every girl should have a best friend, like you're mine."

This is going to be tougher than I thought. "Not exactly. See, I've been at this school a long time. And my number one and number two BFIS positions are, unfortunately, already filled."

Maisie frowns and stops taking notes.

"It's nothing personal, Maisie. If you'd been around all these years, you'd have had a pretty good shot at landing one of these spots yourself. Look at you, you're a great candidate."

Maisie looks at her knees and nods a bit. "It's true. I am."

"And **you should have a number one BFIS who can offer you the time and devotion you so richly deserve,**" I say, bopping her on the chin.

She sniffs and nods a bit more.

"Why, I'll bet we get you a number one BFIS in no time," I say. And I believe it, too. I really think Susannah is wrong. Yesterday in the cafeteria I saw Maisie give all her fries to a fifth-grader spazzing about forgetting his lunch. And then, when the kid scarfed down all the fries and re-spazzed about having no dessert, Maisie shared her glow-in-the-dark yogurt, too. It's quite possible that Maisie hasn't got a mean bone in her body.

"You think?" she asks.

Lethargic

"I know it," I say. "Have you ever given any thought to

Alice Marriott?" I lean closer. "I happen to know for a fact that she can spell *lethargic*."

She shakes her head no. "I'm not a prancing-kitten sort of person."

"Okay. What about Brianna Simpson? **If you can look past the nasal congestion, I'll bet you'll find a really great girl underneath.**"

"The one with chewed-off fingernails?" Maisie asks, wrinkling her nose.

"That's her. **Did you know her father once wrote a book about making cookies without butter?**"

"Really?" she asks.

"Yup. Shortbread, chocolate chip, gingerbread, lemon snaps. All without a speck of butter."

"Wow." A smile moves across her face. Very slowly, she begins to nod. "All right. I'll give Brianna a try."

If You Love Something, Set It Loose in Math Class

With only ten minutes left of fifth period, I figure it's safe to return to music class. Slowly, I take the long way and play a game with myself as I climb the stairs. One step up, one step down. Two steps up, one step down. Three steps up, one step down . . . and so on. At this rate, I should be able to blow off Mrs. Day's end-of-class hissy fit about replacing the instruments silently, since silence equals no dents.

At four steps up, I hear a sighing sound from beneath the stairs. Leaning over the handrail, **I spot a narrow pair of shoes that could only be described as exceptionally ugly bowling shoes.** One of them is tapping. *Tap tap tap tap.* Then they pace.

It's Ian McPherson. Stats: wispy eighth-grader, turns beet red at the mere sight of a female, the founding and only member of Allencroft's math club. As he paces, he tugs on his earlobes and says to no one, "Hi, Cassandra. I'd be honored—no, *thrilled,* if you would go to the Snow Ball with me.

No. No good. Hey, Cassandra, did I tell you I named my hamster after you?"

Let's hope not. "Hey, Ian," I say, heading back down the stairs.

He looks up. With the windows behind him, his little veiny ears become nearly transparent. He adjusts his wire glasses. "Oh, hi, Zoë. I was just, you know, practicing."

"So I heard. Listen, Ian, can I give you a few pointers?"

"I guess. It's not going to cost me anything, is it?"

Hmm. **One day I'll have to give some serious thought to compensation.** This kid's a Trump Industries waiting to happen. "No. My services are free. For now." I walk around behind him and he spins to face me. "The thing is, Ian, you're going about this all wrong. You're too eager, too needy. This girl, Cassandra, is it?"

He nods so hard his glasses nearly fall off.

"This Cassandra is going to think you want her *real* bad."

"But I do! I told her in a cookiegram last week."

I don't know who invented cookiegrams, but every time Allencroft has a cookiegram fund-raiser, I spend the next three weeks doing patch-up jobs on relationships that got stickied up by way-too-sugary intentions. "But you don't *want* to want her real bad! Not in her eyes, anyway. You see, Ian, women are a truly sophisticated species. **We can sniff out the foul stench of desperation two math classes away.** And you know what it makes us do?"

He shakes his head, tugging on his ears again.

"It makes us run into the arms of the next boy who ignores us. If you want this girl to be intrigued enough by you to shop for a cute dress, paint her toenails, and, in Cassandra's case, wax her mustache, you need to make her suffer."

His tiny hamster mouth drops open. "What? Are you sure?"

"Positive. And to undo the damage you did with the cookiegram, I'd suggest ignoring her until three days before the dance. And even then, ask her all casual-like. As if you're bored by dances, and if she is, too, you might as well go and be bored together."

He sniffs. "Three days?"

"Three days."

It's at this very moment I get to see Handsome Mr. Lindsay on a Thursday—a rare treat. Math tools jangling, he walks toward me and Ian. Only instead of waving and walking straight by, he stops and does a laughing little gun-fight thing with his fingers at us.

"Hey there, pardners," he says. "Better get back to class, or I'll run you out of town for loitering."

Ian doesn't like cowboy talk any more than I do and is up and gone in about one and a half seconds.

If Mr. Lindsay were any less handsome, I'd reconsider my plans for him. **I'm not entirely sure I could stand cheeseball comments like that coming from a lesser face.** Especially when they come with freaky cowboy gunplay.

What I'd really like to know is whether or not Handsome Mr. Lindsay has a wife, without making him too suspicious. So, as he follows me upstairs (I don't know what he ever did to deserve the classroom right beside the music room), I casually say, **"Is *Mrs.* Lindsay a math teacher, too?"**

He smiles at this and pulls a picture out of his wallet. **"How did you guess?"** Stopping at the landing, he looks at the photo and shakes his head. "She's the reason I went into teaching in the first place." And he hands me the photo.

I take it, but cannot bring myself to look at it. I'm too busy wallowing in misery. He's not only got a wife, but he loves her so much he became a *math* teacher for her. **Imagine loving someone so much you'd do math every day for the rest of your life, just to make them happy!**

I sincerely hope when I get married, Riley doesn't need me to do any math, because that would be a deal breaker.

"She's a wonderful person," he says. "Still does all her own gardening."

Finally, I glance down. Whoa. She's really very beautiful. A little wrinkly, but all glamorous with her makeup and her fluffy light hair. Also, she's hugging a horse's nose, so I know she rides horses, too. Or at least she hugs their noses.

Teaches math, does all her own gardening, is beautiful, and isn't afraid of horses.

My mom has killed every houseplant we've ever owned, is too tired to wear lipstick, and is terrified of anything with hooves. Not only that, but I once followed her advice about long division and failed my math quiz.

This horse race was over before it ever got out of the starting gate.

Sorcerer's Stands Require Written Permission

The Snow Ball Planning Committee meeting is on the library floor beside the fake fireplace. It's after school and there should be, like, zero chance of us spilling any food on the new lemon-yellow floor pillows.

So far it's me, Laurel, Susannah, Smartin, and the two LameWizards. But they don't count. They never look up except to groan when they lose a match to a goblin or something.

"*Psst,*" Susannah pssts. She leans close and says, **"I've got *major* news."**

"Yeah?" I crawl farther away from the LameWizards so they don't hear.

"I just heard from a Sixer, Jack Muldoon, that your Man-on-One-Knee, **Riley, spent two weeks' allowance on an antique gold necklace**. He's planning to give it to you when he invites you to the dance." Susannah sniffs and rolls her tongue around in her mouth to clear out the Major news.

"Gold?" I ask. "Wow. But wouldn't that cost a whole lot more than two weeks' allowance?"

Susannah snorts and explains, "By antique, Jack might have meant, you know, thrift store. And I never said the gold would be real. Oh, and Riley's going to insist you wear it to the dance so you can be Fred and Ginger."

"Who?" Laurel asks.

"Fred Astaire and Ginger Rogers. They're some famous dancing couple from the olden days." Susannah shrugs. "My mom watches them in old movies and then yells at my dad for never taking her dancing."

Just when I'm thinking maybe Riley and I could become a famous dancing couple, **in comes Maisie with Brianna Simpson, eating chocolate cookies that probably contain zero butter.**

"Hey, Zoë," Maisie says, holding out her cookie. "Want a bite?"

"Thanks, no," I say, smiling.

Brianna starts giggling and bumping shoulders with Maisie. "That totally reminds me, Maisie. Remember . . . Bite? Bite yourself!" And they both crash to the ground laughing. **Personally, I don't see what's so funny.** Also, I don't see how these two could possibly have an inside joke yet, when it hasn't even been two whole days since Brianna became Maisie's number one BFIS.

Unwritten Rule #7. Inside Jokes Require a Minimum of Eight Days of Friendship.

So they're rolling on the floor laughing, spewing butterless cookie crumbs all over the new floor pillows, when I decide, as the Snow Ball Planning Committee chairgirl, that it's time to take control.

"Ahem." **Chairpeople should always begin an announcement by clearing their throats.** Even when their throats feel perfectly clear.

Maisie and Brianna look at each other, burst out laughing, and flop even more on the lemon-yellow pillows.

The nerve! Just when I'm wondering if my chairgirl status allows me to send flopping people to the office, Handsome Married Mr. Lindsay walks in.

"Okay, troops," he says with a whole bunch of hand rubbing. "Let's plan ourselves a dance, everybody. What do you say?"

We all shrug and mumble, "Okay." Inside, I pray he doesn't do the finger bang-bang thing again.

He puts a hand to his ear and says, "What? I can't hear you."

We say, "Okay," a bit louder.

"I can't he-ear you!"

"OKAY!"

Then Mrs. Kettleby, the librarian, scoots out of her office and goes, "Shhhhh!" and some of us glare at Handsome Married Mr. Lindsay. But not me. **I try not to look at him much anymore, because of the whole being-married-and-therefore-no-longer-eligible-to-apply-for-the-husband-job thing.**

"Sorry, Mrs. Kettleby," he says. When he plops down onto a pillow, sharpish math tools scatter all over the carpet, and we hurry to pick them up before someone loses a toe. "Let's go around and each person can give an update on their progress this week. Maisie, how are your plans for the decorations coming along?"

"Pretty good. Zoë says I should paint some snow-covered trees and cover the gym in cotton balls and silver glitter so it looks like a winter wonderland. But it won't be cheap . . ."

"Shouldn't be a problem. We've got plenty in the budget. Laurel, what's cookin' over in refreshments?"

Laurel sits up taller. She glances at me before saying, "After we considered everyone's dietary requirements, we've narrowed our food selection down to a short list. A very short list. And by the way, Zoë, I thought of two more restrictions. Nuts and pesticides."

I beam at her to show what a good job she's doing. **How did I miss nuts?**

"That's what I call teamwork," Mr. Lindsay says with another big clap-and-hand-rubbing event. "And, Martin? What kind of music will we be dancing to at the Snow Ball?"

"The musical stylings of none other than the Brainweeds. My mother hired them for my Bar Mitzvah next year. They're stupid good."

"Stupid good." Handsome Married Mr. Lindsay sticks his bottom lip out and thinks about this. **"Stupid good is all right with me.** Richard? How about ticket sales?"

Richard is one of the LameWizards. For the first time maybe in the whole school year, he looks up and we can see he actually has a very nice face. His eyes seem to be having trouble focusing on us, though. **Maybe he's surprised to see how much bigger and better-looking we all are than his electronic goblins and pixies and tree people.**

"Tickets for the dance will go on sale Friday morning at the Sorcerer's Stand."

Everyone is quiet except for the new BFIS couple—they're just giggling harder.

I was never informed of any Sorcerer's Stand. **Hobgoblin items like Sorcerer's Stands require written permission, which I can practically guarantee I will not grant.** "We don't have a Sorcerer's Stand."

"We do now," Richard says, running behind some bookshelves. "I made it last night out of a refrigerator box." He drags out a huge blue foil-covered box with a window in front and a door in back. It's crawling with drawings of serpents and two-headed dragons and the roof has

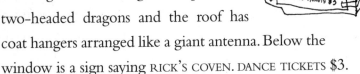

coat hangers arranged like a giant antenna. Below the window is a sign saying RICK'S COVEN. DANCE TICKETS $3.

Handsome Married Mr. Lindsay whistles his approval.

"Who's Rick?" I ask.

The LameWizard smiles, "It's my nickname. Rick." He says "Rick" with a deep voice. Like he's a movie star instead of a LameWizard guy.

Laurel raises her hand even though hand raising is not required at Snow Ball Planning Committee meetings. "My cousin's nickname is Huntie."

"Huntie?" asks Handsome Married Mr. Lindsay. "Unusual. What's it short for?"

"Eliza," Laurel says. This sends Brianna and Maisie into hysterics. They both fall off their floor pillows and onto their backs. They're laughing so hard no sound is coming out.

At this point, I really have to say that **Maisie and Brianna are having way too much fun for a planning-committee meeting.** I mean, Maisie never laughed this hard with me, not even once, and she thought I was her BFIS for two whole weeks! She was wrong, but still! Not only that, she hasn't asked me once today to tell her what Unwritten Rule #10 is. And the whole time I've known Maisie, she's asked me about it seven thousand times a day and I tell her, "All in good time" because I don't want to rush her training.

The whole thing is very vexing. Which means it's very possibly starting to drive me *crazy*.

If I really think about it, maybe getting Maisie a new BFIS wasn't such a good plan. She's completely lost focus on what's really important—her training. With me. I don't want to say I've made a mistake exactly, but I'm going to have to find some way to undo this little . . . slipup.

"I wish I had a nickname," says Maisie. "I'd love to be called Mimsie."

Handsome Mr. Lindsay nods his handsome head. "Mimsie? Interesting. I like it."

He likes it? It's the worst nickname I've ever heard. First of all, **it can't be a nickname if it has the exact same number of syllables as your real name.** A nickname should be shorter. I think I'm beginning to see Maisie's biggest problem.

Her inner thoughts are all messed up.

I know exactly what needs to be done. "Maisie," I whisper. She scoots back from the group and leans closer to me. "I was going to save Phase Two of your training until after the winter formal, but I've suddenly found a hole in my schedule. Are you interested?"

Maisie's eyes light up. "There's a Phase Two?"

There wasn't until about two seconds ago. I smile and put my hand on her shoulder, patting it a little. "Sometimes these things develop as we go along. **I now see Phase Two is essential.**"

"Can Brianna do it, too?"

"No," I say really quick. "Phase Two can only be entered into by one client at a time since it involves an enormous amount of work on the part of the instructor. Which would be me."

"Wow," says Maisie. "Sounds exciting."

"It is." I slide closer to her and squint. **"I need to know what's going on inside you."**

Maisie looks confused. "You mean what's in my stomach?"

"No. Your thoughts. Your innermost thoughts. You do have innermost thoughts, don't you?"

Nodding fast, Maisie says, "Yes. Tons of them."

"Good. I want you to start writing them down."

A smile spreads across Maisie's face. "I can do that. When do I start? Ooh, and can I write about wanting to become an Olympic runner? Because that's my life ambition. Life ambitions are pretty good innermost thoughts, don't you think?"

I seriously don't want to read about running. I'm getting tired just thinking about reading about running. **If I never have to run again in my life, I'll die a happy walker.** "No. Life ambitions are goals and goals aren't private enough. I want you to give me your innermost thoughts on . . ." I chew on my cheek and look around the room. Then my eyes rest on Brianna, who is chewing off her thumbnails. **"On what it means to be a best friend.** One hundred words, and you can start tonight. Okay?"

She bounces up and down. "Okay. First I'm going to say that every girl needs a best friend because—"

"Shh!" I say, and make a zipper motion across my closed mouth. "Write it down. And **have it on my desk first thing tomorrow for editing."**

"Editing?" Maisie squints and tilts her head to one side. "You're going to edit my innermost thoughts? Is that even legal?"

I open my eyes wider and blink. Then I shake my head sadly. "Well, if you don't want to enter Phase Two . . ."

"I do!" Maisie says. "I *so* want to enter Phase Two."

"Good." I smile. "One hundred words—"

"I know. On your desk first thing tomor-row morning."

*T*oward the end of the Snow Ball meeting, to get my mind off the gigantic hole in Martin's sock and the filthy black slime coating his foot underneath, I turn to

Handsome Married Mr. Lindsay. "Does Mrs. Lindsay have a nickname for you?"

His face gets all red and he rubs his cheeks with his hands. "As a matter of fact, yes. **She still calls me Barfy, because I used to throw up when she fed me oatmeal in my high chair.**"

"Whoa," I say, trying to picture how Handsome Mr. Lindsay could have fallen in love with someone who tried to force-feed him oatmeal *and* made him do math. "Your wife must be way older than you if she used to feed you in your high chair."

"What wife?" He laughs. "I was talking about my mother."

Handsome Married Mr. Lindsay is suddenly not so married anymore!

Yes!

What he doesn't know is that he just lost one of his nicknames. He's gone back to plain old Handsome Mr. Lindsay, which is *so* much easier to say anyway.

He Who Swipes the Last Butterscotch Square Has Got to Go

After school the next day, I race the whole way home. I need to go somewhere where I can be truly alone and have a good long look at Maisie's innermost thoughts about being a best friend.

Once I've run into the apartment, said hello to Grandma, and filled my hands with cookies, I crawl under my bed with Maisie's essay, flick on my flashlight, and pull a thick red marker out of my pocket.

What It Means to Be a Best Friend
by Maisie Robbins

Right away, I cross out the extra *b* in Robbins, because I think it should be spelled like the bird. As in, "A flock of graceful *robins*

sits atop the garden gate." That's much better. Then I take a bite of cookie and read on.

To me, being a best friend is the most honored profession in the world. I will be so loyal to my best friend that I won't tell anyone her deepest secrets, not even if I get tortured or worse.

I scratch out this last line. If Maisie expects to move on to Phase Three one day, which I just this very minute invented, I'm going to have to know Brianna's secrets. All of them. They'll be part of the Phase Three collage.

I now understand it is impossible to have more than one number one BFIS, but that I'm allowed to have a number two one day. But under no circumstance can someone ever have a number three BFIS, since it makes the first two look like losers.

I smile here. **Sounds like my little Maisie's growing up.**

It's an invisible rule.

Rolling my eyes and slumping with despair, I cross out "invisible" and write, *I prefer "unwritten."*

I plan to invite only my number one BFIS to my birthday party next month. My mother says we can have a three-layer chocolate chip birthday cake and french fries with gravy and stay up late to watch scary movies.

Hmm. **Chocolate chip birthday cake and fries. Sounds like a good time.** I chew on the end of my red marker for a minute and then draw a big question mark over the entire sentence. At the side I scrawl, *See me after school!*

Inviting only one person to a birthday party seems a bit extreme, even if that person is a number one BFIS. I mean, how much cake can the two of them possibly eat?

All in all, Maisie did a decent job. It was more than a hundred words, but the kid's a bit nervous, this being her first assignment and all. Smiling with pride, I fold up her note and slip it into my pocket. Then I realize something. I should have made a photocopy of her essay before editing it. Once I give this back to her, I'll have nothing for my files.

○ ○ ○

$\mathcal{I}$ crawl out from under my bed and climb on top of it. Just as I'm finishing my third cookie, I'm thinking about how it's too bad I'm not a little kid anymore. When you're younger, moms are in and out of the school all the time—to carry your 3-D Princess-in-a-Tower project, to settle you down if another kid brought balloons for his birthday, to take you home if your nose gets too runny and your teacher's a big wienie about germs. There were plenty of teacher-meeting opportunities back then.

If only I hadn't been too brainless to know I'd need them.

Stuffing the rest of the cookie into my mouth, I uncap my red marker again and pull out a pad of paper to make a list. **If I'm going to get Handsome Mr. Lindsay to marry my mother, it's going to take a little planning.**

Husband-Snaring To-Dos
1. Do something about Mom's hair. Her 'do makes her look like someone's secretary.

And even though she IS someone's secretary, that doesn't mean she has to walk
around advertising it to every single person she could possibly end up marrying.
2. Do something about Handsome Mr. Lindsay's pocketful of math tools. After further
consideration, a sharpened circle-making
thingy pricking my mother between the ribs
could really put a damper on the good-
night kiss.
3. Do something about getting either Handsome Mr. Lindsay to Mom, or Mom to Handsome Mr. Lindsay. Or else, how are they
going to meet?

Just then there's a key-jangling noise in the hallway,
which means Mom's home. Which means spaghetti and
meat sauce can't be far behind.

I carefully tear out my list and hide it where I
keep all other Top Secret documents. The secret
spot is above the head of my bed. It is a small tear in my
wallpaper that I once found and made into a pocket by
sliding a butter knife inside and unsticking part of it from

the wall. The Husband-Snaring To-Dos will be safe in there.

Other Top Secret documents in my wallpaper are things like the pictures Susannah, Laurel, and I took of each of us practicing how to kiss on this gigantic stuffed frog. And a certain poem given to me by the most unbelievably cute boy in the school who happens to be named Riley Sinclair.

The best thing is Dad's picture. The one of me at our secret place.

"Hi, darling," Mom says, coming into my room and kissing me on top of my head. Honestly, if she knew how many greasy-fingered people pat me on the top of my head during the day, because of my being about as small as a rubber boot, she'd probably choose a more hygienic spot. "There's someone here, sitting in the living room. Why don't you go introduce yourself?"

Introduce myself? To our new dalmatian puppy, Spots? I race around the corner and stop dead when I see the someone.

It's a man.

He doesn't see me. He's staring at some papers on the coffee table with a drink in his hand. Like he lives here. And the worst part is, he is *not* Handsome Mr. Lindsay. Immediately, I back up into the dining room so I can pull myself together before I'm stuck actually talking to him. I've had a bit of a shock and I need to adjust my face first.

"Jocelyn," he says, even though Mom is in the kitchen. "Did I mention the part about the monthly extended family Meet 'n' Greet? That's where we invite the whole family down for a night of camaraderie and fun. Kids can come, too."

"Come where?" I say, stepping into the room.

He smiles and extends his hand to me. "Hi there. I'm Jason from Shady Gardens."

Shady Gardens Home for Seniors? I think I tell him my name but I don't shake his hand, since I'm peering down the hall to Gram's door, hoping it's locked. **If he thinks he's leaving here with my grandma tonight, he's going to have to put up a fight.**

Mom comes into the room with a plate of cheese and crackers, which is terrible because it's only going to make Jason from Shady Gardens want to stay.

"Thank you, Jocelyn," he says, looking up at her and winking. At my mother! On the day after I find out Handsome Mr. Lindsay is single!

"No problem," Mom says. "You know, since you live so far out of the city, why don't you stay for dinner? You can tell me more about the facility over meat loaf."

Hey. What happened to spaghetti?

He gets this creepy smile all over his face and he sips from his drink. "Sounds wonderful. An old bachelor like myself never passes up a home-cooked meal."

Suddenly I get the feeling this guy's trying to sell Mom much more than a dumpy beige flowered room for Grandma.

I walk past him to get myself a cracker, and while I'm looking back at him to see if he keeps any sort of tools in his shirt pocket—which he doesn't—the cracker tray tips over onto the carpet at his feet.

"Whoops, Jocelyn! We're going crackers in here!" Jason jumbo-smiles at me like the nurse in the brochure, and then winks like he's saved me from police custody or something.

"Zoë," Mom calls, "can you clean up? I've got my hands full of ground beef in here."

So that is how I get to see Jason up close. Over a pile of crushed-up Ritz crackers. It's not important how they got crushed. Okay, I stepped backward after he jumbo-smiled, mainly because **I've never seen someone smile like that in real life.**

Once I get the mess all cleaned up, Jason hands me his glass and asks me to get him a refill. Which I do. Then he says I did a great job, but could I wrangle up a few more ice cubes, which I also do.

By the time dinner's over, I've gotten Jason one Kleenex, two drinks, three ice cubes, and the last butterscotch square, which I had seriously been planning to put in my lunch for tomorrow.

And he's given Mom not only a stack of dumpy brochures for his beige flowered grandparent jail, but his business card *and* his home phone number. Like she's going to have to call him in the middle of the night to figure out if they serve the old people applesauce on Wednesdays or Thursdays!

After he leaves the house without stealing Grandma, I lock every last one of the front door locks and breathe deep. "Finally," I say to Mom. **"I thought that jerk would never leave."**

"Zoë," Mom says, "Jason is being very helpful, offering

to drive me around the grounds this weekend on his time off. He's a very dedicated man."

Yeah, he's dedicated, all right. Dedicated to stealing not only my grandmother, but my mother as well. And one thing's for sure. **Having Get-me-this-Get-me-that Jason around all the time isn't going to make my life any easier.** This guy needs his own assistant.

And I need Handsome Mr. Lindsay. Now!

No One Can Ever Know
Unwritten Rule #10. Ever

"I need to clear up my schedule if I'm going to fit in extra time to make sure Jason doesn't steal the job away from Handsome Mr. Lindsay," I say.

My girls and I are patrolling the playground at recess, making sure Marcus Owen isn't standing at the top of the hill behind the soccer field and pushing kids over the edge again. So far, we've had to chase him down three times and we've only been outside about eight and a half minutes. "As it is, I've got the two of you"—I pause to smile at Susannah and Laurel so they know I don't consider managing *them* a chore—"who are fully trained, thankfully, then I've got my mother, Grandma, and Get-me-this-Get-me-that Jason. Then there's the Snow Ball Planning Committee, twenty-six classmates, recess patrol, and Handsome Mr. Lindsay. And that's not even including the people that stop me on the way to the water fountain for advice *or* Mrs. Grungen, who has me on a regular moisturizing schedule for Pavel. **Something's got to give."**

"Wow," says Laurel. "All I've got is a little food-coloring issue. I guess I've got it easy."

I wouldn't trade all my duties, including Get-me-this-Get-me-that Jason, **for her blue food concerns**, but I don't say it out loud.

Susannah throws a huge black scarf around her head and face. "All I've got to worry about are the prying eyes of my adoring public." Laurel rolls her eyes and kicks a leaf. Only she misses it completely.

Susannah adds, "Did I mention my agent has gotten me another commercial?"

This is big—Susannah is willing to go back into the public eye. **This is** *huge.* "No, what is it and when?" I ask.

"It's in about three weeks and it pays big, my agent says. It's national. I don't know what it's for, but he said whatever I do, don't cut my hair. He said to take extra-special care of it. So, that pretty much gives it away, don't you think?"

Laurel twists her mouth to one side. She looks none too happy that Susannah is about to be shoved back

into the public eye, not after Laurel's hopes got squashed the first two times. "Maybe they want it real long, so when they shave it off in the military school commercial, your adoring fans get a big thrill."

"Very funny, Laurel!" Susannah snaps. "You're just jealous because your hair is so short from when you dyed it blue and they had to cut it all off!"

"I didn't dye it! **I slipped in Gatorade!"**

Susannah laughs and Laurel looks like she wants to pluck out all of Susannah's hairs, one by one, so I steer them toward the soccer field. Maisie and Brianna are timing each other while they run from one set of goalposts to the other. We watch Maisie, red-faced, tearing across the grass as fast as she can go.

Laurel says, "At least you're done with Maisie. You should have a huge chunk of time now that you're not trying to make over her nasty reputation, right?"

"She doesn't *have* a reputation," I say as we move closer. "Haven't we had this discussion already?"

Susannah laughs and says to Laurel, **"Zoë's very sensitive about her clients.** Don't you know that by now?"

"And who says I'm done with Maisie, anyway?" I ask.

"Just because she times Brianna while she runs doesn't mean Maisie has completed her training with me." And I've got her fully edited essay in my back pocket to prove it.

"Have you told her Unwritten Rule Number Ten yet?" asks Susannah.

"No. It takes a long time to get to Number Ten."

"I'm still waiting," Laurel whines.

"Me, too," says Susannah. "Why won't you tell us Unwritten Rule Number Ten?"

"No one can ever know Unwritten Rule Number Ten. Except me, and even I try really hard to never think about it."

"You mean you're never going to tell us?" asks Laurel.

"She's bluffing." Susannah grins, elbowing me. **"She's just trying to create buzz."**

"Buzz?" asks Laurel.

"Heightened excitement," Susannah says. "Advertisers do it all the time. *I* should know."

We stroll past Bloomer Girl, who's staring down at a clump of rotten sandwich and laughing her head off. She looks up and sees me, then points down, laughing even harder. She's doing such a good job, I slow down and laugh at it, too. To show her she's infecting others with all the fun she's faking. Then I look at Laurel and Susannah, who start fake-laughing, too.

Before we walk on, I wink at Bloomer Girl. And I didn't get that from Get-me-this-Get-me-that Jason. I've winked at people before. Ask Susannah.

Just ahead of us, Brianna, who is sitting cross-legged in the grass, finishes timing Maisie and says, **"Hey, Maisie, it's the Zoë Lama. Maybe she can teach us how to run faster."**

"I hope so," Maisie calls from across the field as she walks back toward us. "Because I'm going to try out for the Olympics one day. And I plan to make it."

"Me, too, only I'll probably make it first since I'm six months older," Brianna says. Then she looks at me. "Can you give me any running tips, O Masterful Zoë Lama?"

I totally could. She pumps her arms *way* too much while she runs. It wastes precious energy. **But I cannot take on another client right now,** so I just smile.

I need to focus on giving Maisie her essay back without anyone seeing. I know exactly what Susannah would say if she knew about Phase Two, which she's never even heard of, since I only just invented it. First she'd say you can't change someone who's bad, which Maisie isn't. Second she'd say if Riley finds out, he'd say I'm going too far again.

"My grandfather was a runner," Laurel says. "Every Friday night he went running with someone named Rosa. She was his running partner. Or maybe his coach."

Susannah and I look at each other.

Brianna laughs and says, "She might not have been his *running* partner . . ."

"Brianna," I say quickly, "I love your running shoes. Snazzy."

"They're okay," she says as Maisie arrives, huffing and puffing, and falls on the grass. "I wanted RaceMakers, but my mom said these were on sale."

As I inch closer to Maisie, I fiddle with her folded essay in my pocket. Maisie says to Brianna, "You're a great runner. You don't need a fancy piece of rubber stitched to white vinyl to get on the team."

"White leather!" snaps Brianna. "How many times have I told you, Maisie, all good shoes are made of leather!"

Whoa. It's beginning to seem that Brianna is going mad. She's never been all that patient, but I've never seen her get worked up into a lather over man-made materials before.

Susannah pokes me in the side and whispers, "Why don't you blow off some of your chairgirl duties onto Brianna? That would free up your schedule and keep her crazy-lady angry fits as far away from me as possible."

Hmm. Not a bad idea. If I handed over, say, overseeing the dance decorations, it might even help me in two ways—less work for me AND more time for Maisie to focus on Phase Two.

"Brianna, I have a little favor to ask . . ."

Brianna doesn't seem happy I'm handing out work, but she doesn't complain too much right away, so I figure I should beat it before she starts coming up with lame excuses, like training for the track team. While she leans over her shoes and wipes at a green scuff mark, I fake a monster sneeze, bending over Maisie and slipping the essay into her hand. She looks down and beams with such joy that I feel a bit like Mrs. Patinkin when she gave me back my vocabulary test last week with a gigantic red "A+" scrawled across the front page.

Just as Laurel asks Brianna to show her how to operate the stopwatch, Susannah nudges me. **"What's with the secret handoff?"**

"Nothing," I lie. "I was returning some work to Maisie. Something I helped her with."

Susannah lowers her glasses enough for me to see a sliver of her eyes. "Come on. Spill."

Real fast, I whisper something about Phase Two, making sure to add in that Maisie practically begged to do it. Which she did.

Practically.

Susannah pushes her glasses back up her nose and laughs. "This should turn out ju-ust fine." Then, as we turn to go, she bends over to pick up the stopwatch, which is now on the grass. "Hey, this thing's cool. I could use this to time my hair conditioning."

Brianna grabs the stopwatch. **"It's not for hair! It's for athletes."** She turns the thing over and shows us the back. "See? It says the Athletic Zone. Because it's for *athletes* only."

"Yeah, I heard you the first time," says Susannah, who doesn't get screamed at by anyone, because of her fame.

"Why don't *you* **try running?"** Brianna asks Susannah. Brianna looks a bit evil when she smiles. "Goalpost to goalpost and back again. I'll time you. We'll see if you can beat my time. Or Maisie's." Then she laughs like it's a physical impossibility.

Susannah steps forward, stands over Brianna, who is sitting in the grass, and bends down. What she does next surprises even me. She lowers her glasses and looks Brianna in the eye. I don't even think she lowers her glasses to look her mother in the eye. As far as I know, it's only ever Laurel or me. "I'm Susannah Barnes," she says. **"I run for no one. I have people. And** *they* **run for** *me.***"**

And with a flick of her cape, she's gone.

Face the Jackals or They'll Eat You Alive

Someone shouts from the edge of the field, "Hey, it's Grandma-in-Pajamas again! The crazy one from the bus the other day!" A bunch of kids race across the playground to the chain-link fence, where, horror of horrors, **Grandma is shuffling along the sidewalk in her footsies** toward the front doors of the school.

This can't be happening. She's coming to get me again?

Is this what she does all day long while I'm at school? Walks back and forth from our apartment door to the locked school door? In her pajamas?

This is very bad for three reasons:
1. Any second now, everyone's going to find out who she is and I'm going to be fried.
2. I'm at school for, like, six hours each day. That's six hours of trouble she could get herself into.

3. Those flimsy footsies are going to wear right through and Mom's going to find out the truth and Grandma's going to be locked up tight.

So what do I do?

"Hey, Grandma," someone shouts. "You better get home before nap time!"

Okay. No one talks to my grandma that way. **If that moronic sixth-grader thinks he can make fun of Gram, he's about to get knocked into next year!** I charge toward him, squeezing my fists. He doesn't have to know why I'm pounding him. I won't give him time to think about it. Besides, I need to shut him up before he attracts more attention to her.

Susannah lowers her glasses and squints from across the field. Her mouth drops open and she races toward me. "Zoë, that's your grandma!"

"I know. I've got to get her home, but first I've got to pound a Sixer." I keep marching toward my prey.

"Don't do it," she says, running along beside me. "Then everyone will know. **You'll be ruined.**"

"I don't care. He made fun of her and she didn't even know it. Gram smiled back." I stop to look at her. "She actually smiled at him. See why he needs his wormy face mashed into the dirt?" I start walking again.

"I do. She's sweet and innocent and he's a rotten, stinking louse. But think about it, Zoë. He's not worth your reputation. She probably can't hear him anyway! She never hears the phone when I call you, right?"

I slow my steps. It's true. She's looking up at the trees without a worry in the world. **Is it really worth facing complete social devastation over one Sixer with a rotten mouth?**

"Grandma's nearly at the school doors," says Susannah. "She'll be inside with the jackals while you're wasting time losing your reputation over an idiot."

This stops me. I spin around to see Grandma getting close to the teachers' parking lot. "I've got to get to her first." I start running toward the school doors. I can cut through the fifth-graders' hallway and stop her before she gets inside.

"And don't worry," Susannah calls. "I'll distract these morons so they don't see you. Your reputation is safe with me!"

Do I love Susannah, or do I love Susannah?

$\mathcal{B}$ursting out of the front doors of the school, I race down the driveway and catch Grandma pausing to peer inside a tiny red sports car. Mr. Stern, our science teacher, is having what the other teachers are calling a midlife crisis. Something about him really hating getting older and balder.

"Grandma," I call, out of breath. "Grandma!"

She looks up and smiles. **"Zoë, honey. Are you all set to go?** Do you have all your homework?"

"Not yet. But it's time we get you home. Aren't you cold?"

"A bit, now that you mention it. If I'd known it would be so windy, I'd have brought my green jacket."

I'm going to have to take better care of her now. Maybe plan out her days so she doesn't have time to think about coming to get me from school. I don't know why I haven't thought of this before. **Grandma needs a busier schedule.**

I walk her all the way to the corner of Allencroft and Beecher, where I stand facing traffic and waving my hands in the air, hoping to flag down a taxicab. Cars and trucks whiz by and after a couple of minutes a yellow cab pulls up right in front of us. I walk Grandma to the door and help her inside. "This nice lady is going to take you home, Gram. Do you have your key?"

She opens her purse and fishes around in it. Then she

holds up a gold key. "This is it. See? It says Key-master right there on the side. That's the one."

"Good."

"But why don't you come back with me, sweetheart? School's over, isn't it?"

Pretty tempting. Just jump in the cab with Gram and pretend the whole thing never happened. But I can't. **I need to show my face so no one knows what happened.** Susannah's right. They can never know what I did and that's that.

"It's over soon. I'll be home in a couple of hours. Get yourself into a hot bath, okay, Grandma? You need to get warm." I give the driver, a nice-looking lady almost as old as Grandma, our address and some cash I had in my pocket for the used-book sale in the library today. And, for an extra three bucks, convince the driver to walk Grandma all the way up to our apartment. Then I race back to school, barely daring to breathe.

Never Trust a Snake

Talk about a good Monday morning. Grandma is having an old friend over to play cards, so I'm pretty sure she won't be doing any sightseeing on Allencroft today. What's more, thanks to Susannah calling all the jackals away from the fence so she could explain just how difficult it is to land a national commercial, **my social status is safe. Nobody saw a thing.**

To make things even better, this morning when I chased Mom to the car with her forgotten purse, she informed me that Get-me-this-Get-me-that Jason—who was supposed to come for dinner tonight to explain more about Shady Gardens' exciting menu—is, in actual fact, not coming! This makes me very happy because yesterday I made a fresh batch of butterscotch squares and now there's more for me and Grandma, who remembered my name all weekend long. And what makes me even happier is maybe Get-me-this-Get-me-that Jason is getting bored with us and is going to find someone else's grandmother to steal and leave mine alone.

I'm starting to think maybe Monday doesn't have a voodoo hex on it after all. Maybe it's all just been a big, ugly coincidence.

Then I walk into the classroom and see Maisie.

It's never a good thing when you find your newest client slumped in a puddle of her own tears. Usually the only one puddle-slumping on a Monday morning is me. But here's Maisie, drooped facedown over the desk that once was mine. Not that I resent being forced to move to the moron colony at the back.

Much.

"Maisie, what's wrong?"

She looks up at me with a face puffed up with tears and no small amount of phlegm. Her bottom lip quivers as she says, **"My dream, my Olympic dream, is finished."** And, with that, she starts sobbing into her crossed arms.

"But you're only twelve. You can't have been rejected by the Olympic committee. Yet," I say.

She shakes her head. "No. I didn't make the Allencroft track team!"

I, myself, would have been thrilled *not* to make the track team, *not* to be forced to run in endless circles every day after school, but it seems insensitive to point this out. "Oh no. **Was it a vinyl shoe problem?**"

"No. It was that snake, Brianna," says Maisie. She clenches her fists. "I hate her! She lied to me. She told me that in the hundred-yard dash I should hold back until the last fifty yards, and then run like crazy. But you know what happened? Everyone else, including Brianna the Snake, ran like thunder from the very first yard. But still I believed her. I thought they'd all get tired around the forty-yard mark and I'd pass them. But they didn't! And I never got the chance to catch up. **Lying is just about the worst thing someone can do. Especially lying a lie that takes someone down.**"

Aha. So Maisie doesn't lie. She couldn't have written that note to Susannah at Lake Labrador. In all my years as the Zoë Lama, I've learned that puddle slumpers are far, far too sensitive to lie about something as important as lying. In other words, Susannah really did get dumped.

"Didn't you tell Miss Dromedary?" I ask. "Shouldn't your coach know about this kind of cruel sabotage?"

Maisie pauses to wipe her nose on her sleeve. "I told her

and she said, 'No reruns. Your time is your time.' See? You can never trust a snake."

"Actually that's Unwritten Rule Number Eight. Never trust a snake."

Maisie doesn't seem to appreciate the coincidence. "Brianna is just about the worst number one BFIS a girl could ask for. She destroyed my future. But what can you expect from a girl with a middle name like that?"

This pricks my radar. I lean forward. "Like what?"

"Brinderella."

"Brinderella? **Brianna Brinderella Simpson? Are you kidding me?"**

She shakes her head.

"What were her parents thinking? It was bad enough that her initials were *B.S.* But they liked Cinderella so much they thought they'd Brianna-ize it? Brianna Brinderella? Are you sure?"

Maisie doesn't look pleased. "Can we get back to me, please?"

"Of course. Sorry. You know what I think?"

"No."

"Remember how Brianna nearly burst into flames the other day, when you assumed her shoes were vinyl?"

Maisie nodded.

"She was feeling guilty over her evil plot to rule the world. Or at least to overthrow you and rule the hundred-yard dash. She knew she'd lose to you and no amount of leather was going to help. The shame must have made her edgy."

"I don't know what I was thinking, trusting her. **What made me think she'd make a good best friend?**"

Anxious to steer this conversation far, far away from the person who actually recommended Brianna Brinderella, I smile and smack my hand against her desk. "It's time to forget about best friendships. Completely. What is it that Oprah says? **When life spits pumpkin seeds at you, it's time to grow sweet potatoes . . . ?**"

Maisie scrunches up her face and shakes her head. "I don't think Oprah would say a thing like that. Maybe Dr. Phil?"

"Whatever. Who said it isn't important. What is important is you and your yams."

The other kids start filing into the classroom and Mrs. Patinkin is already writing something on the blackboard.

"My yams?" Maisie asks.

"It's time for your next assignment," I say. "But this time we're going to focus on something healthier. Forget best friends. Let's focus on . . . boys."

Maisie sits up tall and stops sniffling. "What about boys?"

"The usual stuff. But it doesn't have to be as long this time." I'd like to give the kid a break after all she's just been through. **"Who's your favorite boy and why. Fifty words."**

Just then, Mrs. Patinkin claps her hands and says, "People, take your seats and prepare to reap the knowledge of the day." Then she turns around and says, "Stewie Alan Buckenheimer, get your hands out of that trash can! Your retainer is in your mouth, I can see the metal from here!"

Stewie's dirty fingers fly up to his mouth and start feeling his teeth. "Wicked!" he says, and grins.

As I turn to go back to my desk, I remember something and turn back to face Maisie. "I've got a new red pen to mark your next essay!" But before I can tell her it smells like raspberry Kool-Aid and let her sniff it for motivation, I realize she can't hear me because she's reaching into her backpack for her binder.

"Maisie?"

She still doesn't look back. She's writing down something Mrs. Patinkin is scribbling on the blackboard as if I'm not staring into the back of her head.

Now, I'm all for higher learning—it's something I

encourage for all my customers—but I need a rule to prevent new clients from getting their priorities mixed up.
School might be a necessary evil, but when
you're working with the Lama, the Unwritten
Rules rule. Period.

Don't Build Your Nest on a Flagpole

Sadly, Monday went downhill immediately following puddle-slumping Maisie and is now shaping up to be the second worst Monday of my life. The first worst Monday of my life was, three years ago, the day Smartin pulled up my skirt at the school assembly and cruelly exposed my Sleeping Beauty underwear, which just happened to be the only underwear that came in my size that didn't have ruffles.

This Monday no one bared my underwear, but they bared my soul.

Avery suspects me of stealing his raspberry marker (which is so mine), Maisie suspects me of setting her up with a Sabotage Queen, Laurel suspects Susannah of rigging the Snow Ball King and Queen nominations, and Brianna suspects me of blurting out her middle name over the school PA system. Which I so didn't mean to do.

I was only telling Laurel, who had just finished announcing Snow Ball tickets are for sale at Rick's stupid Sorcerer's Stand.

How was I to know Laurel hadn't turned off the mike?

Not only all of that, but I haven't decided how to tell Susannah that her Never-Been-Dumped reputation is, in actual fact, a sham.

I'm lying on my bed, chewing over the bleakness of my existence, when I hear Grandma in the living room, having trouble opening a bottle of pills. I hurry to help her before she spills the whole bottle onto the floor and I have to spend the next half hour hunting for little pills that rolled under the couch. The TV in the living room is on, showing some kind of disaster with rain-slicker-wearing reporters toughing it out in the drizzle.

"Hey, Gram," I say, crossing the room and sitting beside her on the couch. "I'll help you with that." I pop off the lid and hand her two Tylenols. "Is it your hip again?"

"This body gives me no rest," she says as she washes the

pills down with what's probably cold tea. "If it's not my hip, it's my back. **Getting old is a rough business.** I don't recommend it to anyone."

She points at the TV. "Look at those clowns." I turn to see houses being washed down a hill by a giant rainy mudslide while the house's owners watch with the reporter from far away. "Damn fools," she says.

"Grandma, that's a disaster. It's not the people's fault their homes are being washed away. It's pretty sad."

She snorts and laughs. **"If there's one thing I've learned, it's don't build your nest on a flagpole.** It's slippery in summer and you'll catch your tongue on it in winter."

The messed-up thing about what's happening to Gram is that it comes out of nowhere. You're talking away with her, then—*bam!*—she's not there anymore. I can sort of see how she could get all tied up in her memories, but now she's laughing about families losing their homes. Maybe even their pets. I can't imagine how I'd feel if my home got washed away, but I sure can imagine I wouldn't like people laughing at me.

"Grandma, do you want me to run you a warm bath?"

"There'll be no more hot water. I just gave Lawrence a bath."

See? Now we're back to Dad stories. But I won't complain. **Even blurry Dad stories are better than fun-with-disaster-and-ruin.** I snuggle up closer. "Did he splash water all over the floor?"

She laughs. "He knows better than to do that. We just got back from Auntie Jean's house and he caused quite enough trouble over there!"

Cool. **I love the trouble stories—the more trouble the better.** "What did he do?"

She looks at me for a moment, then leans closer and whispers, "He had a little run-in with one of Jean's Siamese cats."

My eyes are bugging out of my head. I've never heard this one.

"I left him alone in the front room with the cat, and before too long, we heard the animal shooting around the room, knocking over Jean's figurines and yowling. We both rushed in to find Lawrence throwing things at the poor beast." She sits back and shakes her head. "At first we didn't know what he was throwing. Then we saw Lawrence tug on his diaper, shake one leg, and scoop up the little pebbles that fell on the rug. Can you imagine?"

I'm laughing so hard I can barely see. "Poop balls? **He was throwing his poop balls at the cat?**"

"Very distressing." Grandma tsk-tsks. "And up until this morning, I thought he was right-handed." Her eyes close and she sways side to side, smiling to herself.

At that moment the phone beside me rings. I stop laughing when I see from the display it's Mom on her cell phone.

"Hi," I say.

"Hi, honey, I'm on my way home and need to ask Grandma a question. Can you put her on?"

Not while she's still stuck thirty-five years in the past. "Um, no. She's sleeping," I lie.

"Then wake her up. If she sleeps now, she'll be up half the night," Mom says. "Wake her up. I'll wait."

"But I'm right in the middle of my homework . . ."

"Zoë, please."

Just as I'm dreaming up a way for Grandma to have woken up and gotten into the shower before I could stop her, the doorbell rings and I'm *so* saved!

"Sorry, Mom. Gotta go, someone's at the door."

Click.

I yank open the door to see a tall skinny lady with curly

blond hair. She's holding a clipboard and smiling at me like she's a long-lost relative.

"Good afternoon," she says. "Is there a grown-up I can speak to?"

There is, only she thinks she's a bird. "You're gonna have to talk to me."

"Okeydokey, then," she says. **"Have you ever thought about spending a whole day just focusing on yourself?"**

Thought about it? She doesn't know who she's talking to. I *dream* about it. "Sorta."

This seems to please her, because she smiles pretty wide and checks something off on her clipboard. "Do you like neck massages, manicures, and calming Scandinavian mud baths?"

"Sure." **Other than the mud part, what's not to like?**

"What about scalp massage, fresh-squeezed orange juice, and a complete makeover?"

I stand there quietly, wondering what to say. When she just blinks at me and keeps smiling, I say, "What about them?"

"Do you like them?" Her hand grips her pencil so hard, I'm worried she's going to crack it in half.

"Sure."

Another check mark. From the looks of it, I must be doing pretty good on this test.

"Then we're sure you'll enjoy a full day of complete rejuvenation at the Calm'n'Cozy Spa. It can be yours for the ultralow low price of nineteen ninety-nine." She holds up a card saying GIFT CERTIFICATE. Which gives me an idea.

"Can this day of rejuvenation be given to somebody else, as a gift?" I ask.

This makes her even happier and she starts nodding like mad. "Abso-dabso-lutely. We take cash or card. No checks, please. Not unless you're Donald Trump, I always say." Then she leans closer and winks. "You're not Donald Trump, are ya?"

"No."

"Cash or card, then." She smiles.

I don't have a credit card, but I'm pretty sure I've got enough cash. "Hold on a sec. Don't go away!" I tear into my room and stick my hand into my top secret wallpaper pocket. There's a twenty-dollar bill in here I've been saving since my birthday.

Crumpled twenty in hand, I race back to the front door. "Here you go," I say, shoving it onto her clipboard. "One spa day, please."

"Okeydokey," she says. And she fills out my name and address and phone number, then hands me the gift-certificate card. "Just give us a shout the week you want your spa day and we'll get you all set up. Sound good?"

I nod and close the door.

It's exactly what Mom needs to trap Hand-some Mr. Lindsay. A full day of complete rejuvenation.

After I get Grandma her afternoon pills, I arrange my homework on the dining-room table. **Mom says it isn't a homework spot, because it has a good view of the TV.** She thinks it's impossible to watch TV and divide 396 by 42. She's wrong and I've proven it to her many times, but she still says TV and homework don't mix.

Luckily, Mom's not home.

Grandma's fallen asleep on the couch, so I turn the chan-nel to *The Garage Girls* and sit down to start my math. Only, Devon is in the middle of getting her hair accidentally dyed orange on the day of her school prom, so I don't start my math too quickly.

Just as Devon's trying on cool hats to cover the dye job, the phone rings. Our phone, not Devon's.

I grab the receiver while I'm watching to see if Devon

chooses the punky black hat or the lumberjack hat with the earflaps. Then I realize the phone's in my hand and I say, "Hello?"

It's Get-me-this-Get-me-that Jason. "Hello there, Chloe. How are you on this lovely afternoon?"

"It's Zoë. And I'm okay." Devon picked the lumberjack hat, which I think is a good choice since it'll go great with her black boots and party skirt.

"Have you saved me any butterscotch squares?"

Now Devon's taking off the hat and looking at a pair of scissors. She can't! She's got the longest hair of all the Garage Girls, she can't cut it off, even if it's hideous orange!

"I asked if you saved me any squares?"

Jason laughs like he said something funny. Which he didn't.

"No," I say.

"Well, now. That's a shame. Chloe, can you get your mother on the phone for me? I'd like to bring some papers by this evening. So she can get your grandma all signed in."

Get Grandma signed in? I don't think

so! "My mother's not here. You'll have to try back some other day." I start to hang up.

"Wait—do you know what time she'll be home? Because today's the last day your grandma's room is available. After this, I can't guarantee she'll have a view of the beautifully landscaped butterfly gardens."

"That's okay. Grandma's really more of a bird person. Bye—"

"Wait now! Don't forget to tell your mother I'll be coming by around seven with the papers. And tell her I'll be bringing my appetite, so if she's got anything tasty on the stove . . ."

He can't come at seven. **He can't take away my grandma and make her stare at butterflies for the rest of her life.** I have to think of something. "No. Seven won't work," I say. "Don't come at seven."

He pauses for a minute. "All right. I suppose I could make it around seven-thirty—"

"I'll tell her. But **I feel it's only fair to warn you— she's making liver and creamed onions.**"

Jason is completely silent. Not that I blame him. But then he says, "Sounds great. My mother used to make me liver and creamed onions. I'll give your mother a call at work to arrange it."

My head droops to one side. **Of all the billions of people on this planet, we have to find the one moron who actually likes creamed onions.**

$\mathcal{I}$t's 10:15 and I can't sleep. I was so happy Get-me-this-Get-me-that Jason's car had transmission trouble—preventing him from coming—that I offered to clear the table after dinner and secretly finished what was left of Mom's coffee. Now I can't get my knees to stop bouncing up and down on my mattress, either from caffeine or relief. Maybe both.

I jump out of bed and pull the spa-day gift certificate from my secret spot. I was planning to give it to Mom in the morning, but since my legs are running around anyway . . .

"Mom?" I push open the door to find her sitting up in bed reading a book. Her room's all dark except for the one lamp on her nightstand. There's just enough light to see her book's cover. It has this long-haired muscle guy staring into some babe's eyes. She looks like the sort of girl they call a maiden. But no matter what you call her, she seems pretty excited about all the muscles.

Mom puts her book down and yawns. Then she checks the clock. "Shouldn't you be asleep already?"

"I just remembered I got you a present." Climbing up onto her bed, I slide under the covers on Dad's side of the bed and lie back on the big pillows. This I am sure of—there isn't a more comfy spot anywhere in the world.

"A present?" Mom sits up taller and smiles. "But it's not my birthday." Then she looks at me and squints. "Wait a minute, **did you spill pickle juice in the silver-ware drawer again?"**

"No! It's just a gift. For almost no reason at all." I'm holding the Calm'n'Cozy Spa gift certificate behind me on Dad's pillow.

Mom groans. "Almost? Uh-oh . . ."

But then a thought pops into my head. "Mom? Do you ever miss Dad?"

She's quiet for a moment, then she nods. "I sure do, sweetheart."

"Yeah. Me, too," I say. Then I smile and pull out the gift certificate. "This should make you as beautiful as the lady on your book cover." Then I see the maiden again and add, "Almost."

Mom looks confused, then picks up her book and looks at the cover. She laughs and ruffles my hair. "I'm not sure that's possible without extreme measures." Then she takes the certificate from me. "A day at the Calm'n'Cozy Spa! How wonderful." Pressing the certificate against her chest, she squeals and then mashes me against the certificate, which, now that I'm up close and intimate with it, smells like porridge. Mom says, "You did this for me?"

I nod and pick up her book. **"So you can be ready when my new father comes into your life.** Just don't go thinking all the good ones look like this one."

Mom glances at muscle guy and grins. "Too bad."

"Some of the good ones might have shorter hair and maybe even squeaky shoes that don't scuff the gym floor," I say, inching my way out of the bed. I need to escape before I say too much. "It might even be better if a guy *didn't* have all those bulging muscles, then he might have room to keep things in his shirt pockets . . ."

Mom crinkles her nose. "Like what? Pet ferrets?"

Backing out of the room,

I explain. "No. Just regular stuff that's more useful than a bunch of muscles or ferrets."

Muscles and ferrets might help if a burglar was breaking into the apartment or if I had mice under my bed, but this much I know—if I was ever trapped in a roomful of hostile balloons, I'd be reaching for that needle-sharp math tool.

Innermost Thoughts Should Always Be in Blue

Drama class is a gift to kids everywhere. It's payback for all the time we spend sitting at our desks realizing we have absolutely no idea *what* times 9 equals 117 and we may never remember whether the period should be outside or inside the quotation mark.

First of all, the drama teacher is Mr. Slobodian, the nicest teacher with a mustache at Allencroft Middle School. He's got nice brown hair that always needs a haircut, nice floppy-looking clothes, and nice worn-out shoes. He always looks the same. Nice and worn out and comfortable.

And the drama room is the best room in the whole entire building. It's a giant circle, with dark brown bricks for walls and deep circle stairs that step down into the center stage like a giant target. And the best part is, all the floor and stairs are covered in red carpeting, so no matter where you are, you can just lie down and rest. If you need to.

Plus, it's the quietest room. Probably they insulated it

well so Mr. Garson in the gym next door doesn't have to hear our lousy acting.

Mr. Slobodian never claps his hands to get our attention. He just talks and we just listen. It's the weirdest thing.

"Okay, guys, get yourselves into groups of four, gather some props, and come up with a skit involving these three words: *doughnut, ski pole,* and *skateboard.*"

Just like that, Brianna's hand goes up into the air. "Mr. Slobodian. Those are *four* words."

Mr. Slobodian nods and scrunches his lips into a little O. Then he blinks real fast and says, **"Brianna, would you mind going to the office and pretending you're having detention?** It's an acting assignment. Come back when the bell rings."

We all watch in amazement as she happily gathers her sweater and races out the door with her long brown ponytail swinging from side to side. Maisie giggles.

Mr. Slobodian is a genius. Brianna actually thinks she's being rewarded.

Riley, Susannah, and Laurel crawl over and flop beside me on my huge middle step, which is so wide we can all lie side by side and stare up at the acoustic-tile ceiling as we hold our props, which Laurel got for us. Susannah, of course, gets the tiara, Riley gets the broomstick, Laurel gets the drum—which is a mistake. She's never going to stop drumming it, no matter how much we beg. And **I get the fuzzy monkey with ripped out eyes and stuffing coming out of his feet.** It smells like the liners of my winter boots after I get a soaker.

"I've got a good idea," Laurel says, drumming away. "Our skit is about a queen who has no legs, so she gets around her kingdom, or queendom, by sitting on a skateboard and pushing herself with a ski pole. And her doughnut is her crown."

"No way," says Susannah. "I'm not having *no* legs!"

"Why do you always have to be the queen?"

"You want to be the queen?" asks Susannah.

"Maybe," Laurel says. "Maybe I'll even get elected Snow Ball Queen."

Riley looks at me while they continue squabbling and whispers, "Maybe I should be the queen, just to make them crazy."

I laugh. **Riley smells like a real boy. Like baseball mitts and grass and puppies, all mixed into**

one. Wondering how long the gold necklace is, I squinch myself a bit closer and take a deep breath.

Susannah sits up and looks at Riley and me. "This tiara is too jaggedy inside," she says, smoothing her hair. "We need to find me another one, or these sharp pieces of cheap plastic are going to seriously damage my follicles."

Riley, me, and Laurel start to giggle. Follicles? "Why don't you put the monkey on your head? We'll pretend it's your crown," Riley says.

"Or the drum," I say. "If you can get Laurel to stop drumming it." I look at Laurel. "By the way, *please* stop drumming it."

Laurel laughs and keeps drumming.

"Not funny," Susannah says, sort of smiling. "And I prefer the word 'tiara.' What are we going to do? I can't risk a single hair breaking. I'm under contract. Almost."

"An actress needs to suffer for her craft," Laurel says as she bangs.

"Not if she has a good agent," Susannah says. "Then she has people to suffer *for* her!"

Riley laughs. "Don't worry, Susannah. You've always got us for that."

"No way, I need you guys for my posse."

Before Laurel can ask, I tell her a posse is a mob of peo-ple who follow the star everywhere and make it impossible for autograph hounds to get near her.

Just then Maisie crawls over and slaps a piece of paper onto my stomach. "Here you go. I had to write in green, but they're my innermost thoughts, so I hope it still counts."

My Innermost Thoughts on...

♡ Martin

She starts to crawl away, but I stop her. Making sure Susannah's close enough to overhear, I ask, "Maisie? We're playing a game. **Who was your first love and how did it end?**"

Susannah's staring at me with her mouth open and her glasses lifted up. I don't need to see it, I can feel it.

Maisie laughs. "Easy. Donny Wiebe, and he moved to another kindergarten class."

Everyone laughs except me. "Okay, how about the next one?"

She smiles and flops onto her stomach with her chin in her hands. "I had a bit of a dry spell, so the next one wasn't until Lake Labrador. **Susannah, do you remember a chubby boy named Nicholas?**"

Laurel laughs. "You never said he was chubby!"

Susannah's glasses are back in place and her hair covers part of her face. She plucks something hairy from her crown. "I remember him."

Maisie squints. "What a liar he was! **He took me on a canoe ride one night and I pretty much fell in love . . .**"

I'm not sure, but I think I hear Susannah growling.

"And he promised to take me on a hike the very next day. But instead he sent some other girl, Lissy von der Veen, over to my house to deliver a note. It said he had poison ivy, but then later I heard he took *Lissy* on the hike. For the longest time, I thought Lissy set it up, but when she and I got stuck on a ride at the summer fair, she told me the truth. Nicholas was a real skunk."

Then she crawls back toward her group.

Susannah doesn't move at first. She just takes a deep breath. **"He *is* a skunk! A fat little canoeing skunk!"** Then she glances over toward Maisie, who's stuck in a group with Smartin, Avery, Alice, and a LameWizard. "Do you guys mind if I, um, invite Maisie to join in our group? We could use a fifth member."

Riley just shrugs, but Laurel and I smile. We don't mind

a bit. I watch as Susannah crawls over to Maisie, lowers her glasses (!), and motions toward our group.

You gotta love Susannah.

Meanwhile, Riley reaches for Maisie's essay, but before he can grab it, I pull it away and fold it, stuffing it into my back pocket.

"What's that all about?" Riley asks. "Why is Maisie giving you her innermost thoughts in green?"

"I don't know." I laugh and try to distract him by tickling him with my monkey. "I asked for them in blue!"

Riley squints. **"What are you up to this time?"**

"Phase Two of her training. It's no biggie."

"So Phase Two is writing essays on her innermost thoughts in blue?"

"Not every thought. Only the ones I assign."

"Why?"

Sometimes boys are *so* superficial. **How can I work on Maisie's insides if I can only see the outside?**

$\mathcal{I}$ have some official business to attend to, so after drama class I beat it over to the office. Luckily, Brianna's long gone.

I definitely don't want Brianna Brinderella snooping anywhere near my official business.

Both secretaries are on the phone and the office is unusually empty, so I hurry to the machine and place Maisie's green essay on the glass and shut the lid, making sure it only makes one copy. **It would be very bad if anyone found extra copies of her essay** in the recycling bin. The machine whirs and a light shines for a second. Then it spits out a copy that, thankfully, is not green.

I pick it up to read the title. *My Innermost Thoughts on Martin*. Wait a minute. I asked her for thoughts about her favorite boy. Smartin's not a boy. He's a rat!

The first sentence reads, *From the way he laughs to the way he walks, Martin Granitstein is the most darling boy at Allencroft Middle School.*

The way he laughs? Most times he's got milk spurting out his nostrils! And he walks like one shoe is filled with syrup, which it usually is! Did I not inform her of Unwritten Rule #3, which clearly states that Smartin is vile? I'm beginning to think I've failed Maisie. I've let her risk her own reputation by falling for the wrongest of all the wrong boys. I should have seen it coming.

Because if there's one single thing that will surely destroy even the most solid reputation at Allencroft Middle School, it's publicly declaring your love for Smartin Granitstein.

Libraries. Not So Hazard-Free Anymore

It's not even four o'clock and already it's been a roller-coaster ride of a day. And I hate roller coasters. This morning my mother was heading off to the Calm'n'Cozy Spa. She is probably lying in a Scandinavian mud puddle getting gorgeous this very moment. In other words, by the time she gets home, she's going to look seriously hot. Which is excellent, because I could use a bit of good news, since my trainee (whose Lake Labrador reputation has been cleared) has suddenly lost her mind and Riley thinks I've lost mine.

Speaking of Riley, **I'm wondering if my own wedding is a fantasy. If the groom thinks you're nuts, there's a good chance he's going to be a no-show.**

On my way into the library for our dance-committee wrap-up session—the Snow Ball is in three days—I bump into none other than Ian McPherson of cookiegram fame.

"Hello, Miss Lama," he says with a bow worthy of a prince. A nervous prince, but still a prince. "I want you to know, I've taken your advice. I haven't so much as glanced in Cassandra's direction in days!"

"Cool," I say.

"Just yesterday in math class, she came up to me and asked for a pencil." He chuckles and hangs his head to admire his bowling shoe. "I almost fell for it, too. Almost gave her my spare Stylo 2000 Mechanical Click. But then **I remembered what you said about women sniffing out the foul stench of desperation and I held my ground.**"

Ooh boy. This guy's taking my advice wa-ay too literally. "You mean you wouldn't share your pencil? What did you say?"

He puffs up his sunken chest and grins. "Shook my head and said, 'Nah.'" He laughs and holds out his hands for me to give him a high five. Which I do, in spite of a lifelong detestation of fives, both high and low. "Just like that," he says, laughing. "Nah."

"Ian, I'm not entirely sure you got my drift," I say carefully. "If the girl needs a pencil, give her a pencil. I just meant . . ."

He waves to me as he trots away backward. **"I've already bought my tuxedo. Light green!"**

Oy.

*H*andsome Mr. Lindsay looks confused. "Laurel, how did we spend nearly three-quarters of our budget on refreshments?"

She looks at me and fidgets with her hair. "We had pretty tight food restrictions. So everyone would feel included, like Zoë said. Then Zoë said everything needed to be organic and I discovered I could only buy supplies at Le Chef Organique, which is kooky expensive. When I saw all the fancy choices, I didn't know whether I should buy local foods or not. Finally I decided not, because the foreign stuff had cooler names."

Handsome Mr. Lindsay's eyebrows are sinking lower and lower as he listens.

"By the time I found Zoë's gluten-free ginger cookies and the berry-infused sparkling water, my mother started honking in the car and . . . well, I went a little over budget. Sorry." Laurel looks down at her lap.

Handsome Mr. Lindsay coughs. "Well, it certainly sounds like Zoë took her duties as chairwoman quite serious—"

"I, um, it's chairgirl," I almost whisper.

"Chairgirl," he says. "I can only assume our chairgirl won't mind staying after the meeting to help poor Brianna, Maisie, and Martin get creative with what little remains in their budgets. Can we count on you for that, Miss Chairgirl?"

"Um, yeah. Okay."

"Thanks a lot, *chairgirl*," says Brianna under her breath. "There goes the silver glitter." Really, I think she's being a little dramatic about this whole Brinderella thing. I didn't *name* her, after all. **She should direct this hostility at her parents.**

"And another thing," Handsome Mr. Lindsay says. "Due to unforeseen budgetary constraints"—he pauses to look at me—"the Snow Ball King and Queen, who will be elected tomorrow during morning recess and crowned at the dance, will still have crowns, but no red velvet robes. I'll have to return them."

Uh-oh.

Susannah sits perfectly still. Then **her mouth tightens into an angry little slash** and from deep inside her comes a faint, faraway rumble—like a panther ready to pounce on a mouse.

$\mathcal{I}$'m not really listening to Handsome Mr. Lindsay talk about dress codes for the dance.

Because no matter what, I'm wearing my lavender dress that looks like a slip because it'll go really well with Riley's gold necklace. And besides, I have to think about how, exactly, to get Handsome Mr. Lindsay delivered to my apartment tonight to see my fancy shined-up mother.

It can't wait until tomorrow. **I've ordered a bunch of flowers for Mom with a romantic card from Handsome Mr. Lindsay,** and flowers wilt. Plus, Mom arranged for Get-me-this-Get-me-that Jason to come over tomorrow instead of yesterday. Besides, Mom's relaxation might have worn off by then.

I never thought the idea would come from Handsome Mr. Lindsay himself.

"When I saw all the girls in those platform shoes at Middleton School that year, I knew we were headed for trouble," he says. "And sure enough, there I was, an hour later, carrying one of them to the hospital with a sprained ankle. So definitely *no* platform shoes at the Snow Ball. Laurel, will you make the announcement tomorrow morning?"

Laurel nods.

That's it. **All I need to do is appeal to Handsome Mr. Lindsay's hero instinct by spraining my ankle in the next half hour.**

Shouldn't be too difficult.

As the rest of the committee debates the dangers of poorly attached spaghetti straps, I get to work on my plan.

The thing is, I've never actually sprained a body part before, so I'm not sure how to do it. **I'd like to keep the agony to a minimum, if at all possible.** I could let someone's chair leg come down on my foot. But that wouldn't be easy unless someone lifts their chair for some reason and I can throw myself underneath it real fast. Or I could wander off in search of a book on making punch— we are in a library, after all—and pull a big display case on top of myself.

But that seems a little dramatic.

As I gaze around the room, I realize with great sadness that there is very little opportunity to sprain oneself in a school library. Other than the odd paper cut, you're looking at a fairly hazard-free zone. I'm going to have to injure myself in the hallway.

Slowly, silently, I lean back in my chair and peer through

the open door. There really isn't much out in the hall except a bulletin board and a janitor's mop. **Basically, I'd need to run full force into the cement wall to injure anything well.** At least the office is right next door, in case I misjudge and crack so many bones that Handsome Mr. Lindsay has to call for help.

Comforted by the invention of 911, I smile to myself. I'm a genius. I'm this close to being flower girl at the wedding—

Suddenly my chair slips out from under me. It screeches forward and I fly backward, way faster than I'd ever have planned. I'm hanging in the air for what seems to be about a whole minute.

Then the floor rises up and I feel a sharp crunch in my elbow.

$\mathcal{I}$t was really nice of Handsome Mr. Lindsay to volunteer to take me to the hospital, since Mom wasn't home when we called her and her cell phone was turned off. And it was really nice of the nurses to distract me with teen magazines while the cast was going on.

So I guess my plan worked. Here I am in the back-seat of Handsome Mr. Lindsay's Honda with a handful of

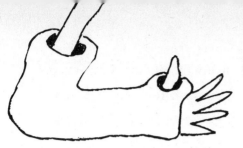

pullout heartthrob posters and we're headed straight for my apartment.

In the elevator I'm so excited I could burst, but Handsome Mr. Lindsay chalks it up to the pain medication. **Mom should be in a terrific mood after all the calming mud baths.** She'll probably look as beautiful as she did before I was born; back when she, as she says, "had time to fuss with silly things like makeup and hair dryers." I can't wait for him to see her. I'm going to hide in the kitchen and spy until he kisses her!

When we get to the eighth floor, I goof. I almost call him Dad. As the elevator door opens then suddenly starts to close on us, he puts his arm across it so it doesn't slice me in half. The guy risks his own flesh for me, so, like an idiot, I go, "Whoa! Thanks, Da—Mr. Lindsay." Just like that.

I'd better be careful. He won't want to marry my mother if she has an overly needy kid. It's bad enough I'm a budget wrecker and an elbow cracker. I smile at him as we approach my apartment and imagine him coming through the door each night, emptying his pointy math tools on the hall table and running to find me and tickle me before he bakes us some cookies. Chocolate chip.

"This is it," I say, pulling out my key. "The lock works pretty good. My key almost never gets stuck." I show him—just so he knows living here won't be a hassle—and I push the door open. "You'll like my mom; she was prom queen before she got too old."

But as soon as the door is open, my happiness fades away, replaced by immediate horror. I don't know what kind of spa that place is, but Mom doesn't look relaxed or rejuvenated. She's lying on the couch in wrinkled pajamas, with a HUGE red nose, hair in every direction, and a mountain of dirty Kleenex on her lap.

One thing's for sure. Handsome Mr. Lindsay isn't going to be kissing her tonight. Maybe not ever.

"Zoë, honey," Mom says. "Are you okay? I just got home and spoke to the hospital on the phone." She tries to sit up, but falls back onto a pillow, moaning like a wounded cow. "I'm afraid I've got the flu."

"That's okay, Mrs. Costello," Handsome Mr. Lindsay says, bringing me inside. "Don't get up. Zoë's going to be just fine, aren't you, kiddo?"

Suddenly my arm throbs. I just want to go to bed. "Yeah," I lie. "I'm terrific."

Handsome Mr. Lindsay walks across the room and holds out his hand to shake Mom's, but he pulls it back when she sneezes into a clump of used tissues. "I'm Matthew Lindsay," he says, stepping out of the way of the flying germs.

"Lindsay?" Mom sits up taller and looks at my flower delivery, which is on the coffee table with a small card lying beside it. Opened. **"Are you the Mr. Lindsay** who **sent me these beautiful flowers?** They just arrived."

He holds up both hands and laughs. "No, ma'am."

Mom looks confused. "That's strange. You're the only Mr. Lindsay I've ever met. And the phone number on the card is the school's number."

They both look confused. Then **they both look at me and suddenly I think maybe *I* have the flu.** What was I thinking?

Mom notices his shirt pocket filled with math tools instead of ferrets or bulging muscles and I realize I'm *so* busted.

"Zoë," Mom says, "do you know anything about this?"

Handsome Mr. Lindsay stares at me with a weird smile on his face. The kind of smile someone might smile if they think they've swallowed a centipede. I'm so embarrassed, I could die. He must think I'm a total and complete idiot!

I step backward. "I seriously don't think you should be questioning me right now. **I've had a bad fall and the doctor said I need my rest.**" Spinning around, I rush down the hall to my room, where I can bury myself in blankets. I must have been insane to plan this. Insane! Just before I shut my door, I hear Mr. Lindsay telling Mom his number one policy. He never, ever dates parents of his students.

Figures. The first guy I pick for Mom has "policies."

It's time to pull out Unwritten Rule #12, which I'm writing in my head this very minute. **Hooking Up Your Mother Is a Dead Duck Waiting to Happen and Is, from This Moment On, Illegal.**

It Ain't Over till the Lady in White Sings

The next morning I can't figure out how to get my coat on over my cast, so I completely miss the school bus *and* a ride from Mom, but not in that order. So I'm forced to scrabble my way to school with my hot-pink cast in a sling, but otherwise bare, and a coat and backpack hanging from the other shoulder. The coat keeps slipping down to my elbow, taking the backpack with it, and every three or four steps I trip over the whole mess.

Advice to self: don't break any more elbows at the end of November. And if you stupidly ignore this advice, buy yourself a cape as soon as the plaster dries.

It's not helping one bit that the whole husband-snaring attempt has officially backfired. My mom has rebooked her Calm'n'Cozy beauty day for a week from Thursday. So now she'll look beautiful for exactly no one but me and Grandma. Not that it matters anymore, not since Handsome Mr. Lindsay has flipped-out rules about dating and is seriously paranoid about sneezes.

Did I mention I'm never fixing up another mother of mine? Ever?

Now that I'm injured, I'm in desperate need of not one, but two, assistants. And maybe even a taxi service. I reach down to pull my jacket up for the millionth time. I'm also in desperate need of that cape.

What I'm also in desperate need of is a ten-foot pole to keep Get-me-this-Get-me-that Jason from entering our apartment. He's due to arrive tonight at seven sharp, Grandma-stealing papers in hand.

As I'm tripping my way across the school playground, I see Maisie running for the door. She's late, too. "Maisie," I call, "hold the door."

She holds it and smiles when she sees my cast. "You got the pink! I bet Laurel my chocolate milk you'd get the pink. She wanted you to get the—"

"They were out of blue," I say, staggering inside the school. "I'm glad I bumped into you. I was . . . kind of surprised to read your essay."

She beams and unzips her jacket as we walk to class. "It was exactly fifty-one words. I counted." She pulls off her hat and smiles. "I was hoping I'd get extra points for going over word count."

"Yeah, word count wasn't the problem . . ." She's such a nice kid; I don't know how to break it to her that she flunked her latest assignment. Maybe I'll tell her at recess. I could share my butterscotch square before I hand back her essay, to sweeten the blow. As we get closer to our classroom, we're stepping over white papers. Everywhere, on the walls, on the lockers, on the floor, are white sheets of paper. **Kids are pouring into the hallway, all of them clutching white papers and shrieking.** Comments come from beside us, behind us, in front of us . . .

"Did you read it?"

"I'm gonna heave!"

"Is she here yet?"

"Gross!"

Two older girls reading from a paper pass by us and burst out laughing.

A fifth-grader sees us and stops dead. Then he tears back the way he came.

The Sixer couple who always make out by the garbage Dumpster look at Maisie and mumble to each other. Then the girl clutches the guy's face and screeches, "Oh, Martin. Kiss me now!" Only her boyfriend's named Rodney.

I'm getting a very bad feeling.

"What's going on?" Maisie whispers to me. "Why are they making fun of us?"

I shrug, dump my coat and backpack to the floor, and grab one of the papers floating around us. I turn it over and gasp. How can it be?

It's Maisie's "I Love Smartin" essay.

Dropping to the ground, I grab another. And another. They're all the same. **The school is snowing "I Love Smartin" essays.**

Uh-oh. An even worse feeling is suddenly replacing the very bad feeling . . .

Could I have left the original in the copy machine? I don't know; I can't think! I look up at Maisie.

She's got two handfuls of essays and is looking at them one by one, her face horrified, and throwing each down to the ground. Eyes wide, mouth gaping, she looks at me and whispers, "What did you do?"

"Maisie. Believe me, I would never—"

"You set me up."

"No! It was an accident. I swear!" How could I have been so stupid? So careless—

"You lied to me. You were never helping me at all!"

"No, I swear—"

"How could you do this?" Maisie steps backward, glaring at me. "I *hate* you, Zoë. I hate you. You've destroyed my whole life!"

"Maisie, wait!" I watch her run down the hall as I sit in a lump, legs sprawled out in front of me, surrounded by proof. She's right. I really have destroyed her life.

For once, I have no answers.

Then, from the crowd of whispering kids, out steps Bloomer Girl. Allegra of no-one-wants-to-play-with-me fame. Her tear-covered cheeks are pinker than my cast and she folds her arms across her chest. "Nice advice, Zoë Lama! I did what you said, made like I was having tons of fun, and now **the entire fifth grade is calling me Schizo-Chick!** They think I talk to myself!" She spins on her heel and slips on a love letter as she stomps away. "Remind me never to ask your advice again!"

"Allegra, don't go!" I call. "I didn't mean for that to happen—"

"Did you mean for THIS to happen?" Ian McPherson is stumbling toward me waving two torn-up dance tickets. "I waited until three days before the dance, just like you said.

And then I asked her, just like you said. And do you know what she said?"

From the look on his face and the way my day is going, I can probably guess, but I shake my head anyway.

His little eyes flash with anger from behind his glasses and his ears stick out so far I almost wonder if they'll pop off. "She said no. And you want to know why?"

I really, truly, would rather not.

He squeezes his little rodent lips together before shouting, "She said she thought I wasn't going to ask her, so she agreed to go with Kevin Franklin. KEVIN FRANKLIN!"

My eyes are starting to sting as I try hard not to cry. He really should have loaned her his Super Mechanic Stylo or whatever it was. **I try to wipe my nose with my sleeve, but I scrape my face with my cast instead.** And now my elbow really hurts.

Laurel and Susannah have shuffled closer. But they look like they're not sure they should admit to knowing me.

Then a howl of laughter and whistling explodes from the other end of the hall, where someone, someone white-haired and tall, is wandering along all by herself. It's hard to see her through the crowds of kids, but she's carrying a red purse and wearing . . . **Oh no! Pink footsie pajamas!**

It's Gram!

"Which one of you children can tell me where my granddaughter's classroom is?" she says as her head bobbles side to side. "It's time to take her home."

I stand up. Love letters fall from my lap.

Laurel puts one hand on my good arm. "Zoë, stay put! They don't know who she is yet."

"She's that old girl from Allencroft Boulevard!" someone shouts. "Grandma-in-Pajamas!"

"Hey, Grandma! Wanna dance?" shouts an eighth-grader.

Grandma beams and takes the jerk's hands, letting him twirl her around as the whole school laughs at her. She laughs, too. She thinks they're laughing with her. One of her footsies, I can see now, is torn away from her bare foot. Kids are pointing, laughing harder.

My heart sinks into my stomach. The whole neighborhood's going to find out about this. My mother's going to hear for sure. And if Mom hears, Get-me-this-Get-me-that Jason will hear and everybody will say the same thing—it's time. I start walking toward her, pulling my arm away from Laurel. Susannah grabs at me. "Zoë, no!" she whispers. "I can take her to the office. No one has to know! Think about your reputation!"

With a sad smile I push Susannah's hand away. "It's a little late for that, don't you think?" I walk, then run toward my grandmother. I push the eighth-grader away from her and take Grandma's arm in my cast. Then, in front of the whole school, I say, **"Come on, Grandma. Let's take you home now,"** and guide my beautiful old grandmother through the gawking crowd.

Don't Paint Spots on a Leopard

When we get home, I get Grandma changed into regular clothes and into bed for a nap. Then I sleepwalk to my room, where I flop facedown on my pillow. I've never been so tired. So worn out.

So alone.

I just need a little . . . sleep.

I open my eyes and blink. I don't know how long I slept, but my room is completely dark. I have a sick feeling, but I don't know why. Then it all comes back to me. **Thoughts come gushing, pouring, flooding back into my head. And they all say pretty much the same thing.**

My life is over. I always knew that the moment my advice failed me, the moment my reign ended—and, boy, did I end it today—my own reputation would be smashed apart. Which is pretty much how I feel.

But I don't have time to think about that now. It's nearly six o'clock and Grandma needs her dinner before Mom comes home with McDonald's for me. Just to make this day complete, Get-me-this-Get-me-that Jason is coming tonight to see my mother.

"Grandma," I holler as I start flinging open cupboard doors. "Do you want macaroni or tuna fish?" She doesn't answer, so I pull a can of tuna from the cupboard and open it up. "You know what they say about fish, Grandma? They say it makes you smarter because of the schools. You know—schools of fish?"

She still doesn't laugh or answer, but I can hear the TV going, so I go see what she's watching. In the living room, I find *Jeopardy!* on the TV, but Grandma is lying very still. Her mouth is gaping open.

"Grandma?"

She doesn't wake up. I walk over to her and shake her shoulder. "Grandma?" **Her hand, which had been lying on her stomach, drops onto the couch with a thud.** A very heavy thud.

"GRANDMA!" I shriek into her ear.

Her eyes fly open and she sits straight up. "What the Helen Hunt are you doing?" Her hand starts patting around the couch cushions, looking for her teeth. Normally I try to avoid touching them, but I pick them up off the floor and place them in her hand. "I thought you were . . ."

"Dead? **Can't I take a nap anymore, without strangers pulling out a shovel?**"

"But . . . I'm not a stranger, I'm your granddaughter."

She tilts her head and stares me up and down. "But I don't have a granddaughter. Only a son."

I don't know what it feels like to take a punch in the stomach, but I feel like I've been punched. And hard. **Why am I not worth remembering?** All those mornings with the crossword puzzles and the cocoa . . . how can she have just forgotten them? I know she can't help it and I shouldn't take it personally, but it's nearly impossible not to when you're the only one in the family being forgotten. I'm trying to decide if I should explain this to Grandma when I hear water. Not dripping either. More like pouring and splashing.

"Is Mom home?" I ask, walking toward Grandma's bathroom.

"I'm pouring myself a little bath," she says. Which makes me run, because she was sound asleep for who knows how long when I came into the room!

Pushing open the bathroom door, I step inside, and instantly my feet are under water. No! Mom's gonna freak, because the bathtub faucet is on full blast and steaming water is pouring out of the tub, all over the tile floor! As quick as I can, I turn

off the tap and reach in to pull the plug even though water spills out way *worse* when I stick my arm in.

I yank every towel off the towel rack and throw them on the floor, but not before water starts pouring out into the hall. Racing to the closet, I fill my arms with every single towel and sheet I can find and throw them everywhere to sop up the mess, which is *massive*.

At this very unfortunate moment, someone knocks at the front door. **I don't want anyone to see the lake that is now our bathroom.** At least it can't be Mom, since I know she remembered her keys; I gave them to her on her way out. I go peer through the peephole with one eyeball and see the building superintendent's eyeball staring back at me.

It looks huge. And mad.

"You got a problem with your bathroom?" he asks as I open the door a little. "Because the Burtons below have some water dripping from their ceiling."

I can't tell him. It'll cost Mom heaps of money and she'll only hurry faster to send Grandma away. Hiding my wet feet behind the door, I say, "Our bathroom?"

He narrows his eyes and tries to look past me down the hall, like maybe he's going to see a tidal wave coming at him. "Yeah. You got a leak?"

"Um . . ." I start to say.

He puts a hand on the door and starts to step inside, but I block the door with my foot. "Sorry. My mom's not here and I'm not allowed to have anyone over until she gets home." That was quick thinking.

He makes a hissing sound and steps backward. "Tell your mother to call me as soon as she gets home. We got a real mess down below."

I nod and shut the door fast. **I'm *so* not telling her to call him when she gets home.**

By the time I get back to the bathroom, the tub has stopped overflowing and is making happy gurgling drain sounds. Only I'm extremely not happy. All around me are sopping towels and if I don't get them dried before Mom gets home, she's going to say Grandma's going downhill and there's no more time to waste.

I don't want to hear those words; even if my wet feet and the footsie pajamas are proof they're true. As I pull off my socks and hurry to Mom's room to look for quarters for the dryer, I realize something that makes me want to go back to my pillow.

Dr. Milner isn't the biggest idiot of the geniuses I'd hoped he was.

After I get everything dry and put away and get Grandma fed, I check the phone book and call every Robins I find. I don't have much luck until I remember that Maisie spells her name wrong, with two *b*s. Then I call everyone named Robbins. The very last number—for Robbins, W—is Maisie's.

Her mother answers. "Hello?"

I try to make my voice as casual as possible. "Hi. Is Maisie there, please?"

I hear a muffled sound. It sounds an awful lot like Maisie's mother's hand covering the receiver. Then she comes back on and says, "May I tell her who's calling?"

"Zoë. From school."

More muffled sounds. Then **I hear Maisie say she'd speak to anyone in the solar system *but* me.** I think her mother argued with her, but it doesn't really matter. Before she comes back on the phone to give me the bad news, I hang up.

No one is home but Grandma and I need someone to talk to, so I tell her the whole story. Starting with Maisie's old reputation and ending with me messing up everything. For a minute, Grandma looks like she understands what I said. And by the way she's looking at me, tilting her head with watery eyes, I'm almost sure she knows me. That I'm not a stranger, but her actual granddaughter.

But then she says, "Don't try to paint spots on a leopard." She turns back to face the TV and I realize I was wrong.

Grandma wasn't home after all.

*M*om walks in soon afterward. She plunks my chicken nuggets on the dining-room table and says a quick hello to me and Grandma before heading straight for Grandma's bathroom. That's also the guest bathroom and she probably wants to get it ready for Jason. About three seconds later she says, real loud, "Ugh! Zoë, what's this puddle beneath the shower curtain?"

So all my cleanup work was pretty much for nothing, because at that exact moment the phone rings and I can tell from Mom's face that it's the building superintendent. She keeps saying, "Oh no. Oh *no*," and looking back and forth from Grandma to the bathroom. Finally she hangs up and slumps into a dining-room chair. She's shaking her head and tapping a finger on the table. Then she drops her head into her hands and massages her temples with her fingers. By the time she looks up, her hair's poking every which way and she reaches for two things.

Jason's business card and the phone.

I head for my room. I don't want to hear what she's going to say. But just as I'm closing my door, I do anyway.

"Jason? It's Jocelyn. I just wanted to remind you to bring the application papers."

If You Gotta Jump, Take No Prisoners

In the middle of the night, I wake up terrified and sit up fast. My heart is pounding and I'm gulping to breathe. I've been dreaming about Maisie and Smartin, only instead of millions of love letters blowing around the school, there were millions of pictures of me. Everywhere.

Grandma was there, tucked into a beige flowery bed, and she and all the kids were laughing at me. Not a single person cared about my rules. I was the Zoë Lama no more. My reign was over.

Just like real life.

I sit there for a few minutes, clutching my blankets to my chin and blinking in the dark. Then a really bad good idea pops into my head. Really bad because it's the last thing on Earth I'd ever want to do. And good because it's the only way to make things right for Maisie.

Settling back on my pillow, **I work on a plan that is, no question, going to destroy me.**

○ ○ ○

*I*t's lunchtime. I'm sitting in my usual spot. At the middle table in the very center of the cafeteria. With a tray full of hamburger and fries and chocolate shake in front of me and Laurel and Susannah on either side. But **delicious food can't help me today.** Neither can the two best friends in the world.

From every direction, people are pointing at me, whispering and giggling. But that's okay. It doesn't matter anymore.

I'm about to do something so ferociously wrong, so entirely against the laws of nature, that even my BFIS one and two are sure to be done with me forever. In fact, I'd *recommend* it.

The noise of kids mocking me is deafening. And outside it's raining, so we had indoor recess this morning. Which means the kids are extra riled up; throwing milk cartons and raisins at one another while the lunch ladies run around trying to stop it and getting hit in the head in the process.

Laurel, who brought her own lunch, licks her empty blueberry yogurt container. "So, Susannah, when's the big day? When's the commercial?" Laurel is good people. Even if it kills her to hear about Susannah's next shot at fame, she's trying to pretend what's happening around us isn't happening.

Susannah smiles and flicks her hair behind her shoulder, where it won't get messed up by her burger. "Tomorrow. I get to miss the whole morning because I'm going to my agent's first to sign some papers."

"Lucky," grumps Laurel, who never gets to miss a school day for anything, on account of her mother being a high school principal and having strict . . . principles.

I push back my chair. It's time. Being extra small, I climb on top of my seat so everybody can get a good look at me while I make my announcement. **If I'm gonna do this, I might as well do it big.**

"Zoë, get down!" Susannah says, tugging on my pant leg. "You're going to get hit by raisins."

I wave her away and clear my throat. Only the place is too loud and crazy for anyone to hear my signal, so I decide to be more forceful. "Ahem!" I say, real loud. A few kids stop and look at me, but the food fight continues. "AHEM!" I say even louder. The noise trails off into silence and I get a little dizzy when **I feel about six hundred eyes staring at me.** Sucking in a deep breath, I begin.

"In light of certain letters that have been plastered around certain schools—letters about certain people—I have a certain announcement to make." I pause to sip my milk shake, hoping the chocolate will stop my hands from shaking. "But I warn you, what you are about to hear might come as quite a shock, and many of you will feel a certain amount of revulsion. **If any fifth-graders would like to leave the room, I recommend they do it now.**" No one leaves the room, but an empty milk carton flies by my head and clatters onto the floor behind me.

"It was *my* love letter," I say. All around the room, kids and lunch ladies gasp. "Yes, it's true. I am, in actual fact, in deep, deep love with SMARTIN GRANITSTEIN."

Laurel and Susannah both say, "No!" and Smartin stands up, punches both fists in the air and shouts, "YES!"

Everybody else groans in disgust and makes throw-up sounds.

I continue. **"I can no longer contain myself, as MY LOVE IS TOO STRONG."**

"Shut up, Zoë!" Susannah pleads. "You're destroying yourself!"

Tables begin to rock with laughter and raisins pelt me in the knees. "Smartin Lover!" someone calls out. I hope I'm wrong, but I think it was a lunch lady.

Clapping my hands, I try to restore order, but it's not easy with Smartin stomping across the tabletops, beating his chest like an ape. "Quiet now!" I shout. "I haven't finished. The letter you all found might have had a certain new girl's name signed at the bottom. But she is not to be held responsible. For it was I, in a fit of passion I could no longer keep to myself, who signed it Maisie. **My passion overtook my senses.**"

A roar fills the room. I try not to vomit when I see Smartin standing on the window ledge waving to the eighth-grade boys, who cheer him and whoop their congratulations.

"So please," I shout over his filthy gloating, "forgive Maisie! **It is I who must shoulder this burden alone.**" I bow my head in shame and raise my hands in the air. "Do with me what you will."

Laughter is practically shaking the room and I fear my plastic chair might tip. Wiping ketchup from my face, I climb down and make my way to the door, holding my cast over my head to deflect the hamburger patties and balled-up napkins.

The last face I see before passing through the door is Riley's. I look at him and, for a moment, remember his plan—the getting down on one knee and the necklace. I want to say something. Anything. But it's too late. He's already turned his back on me.

Pay No Attention to the Unwritten Rule Behind the Curtain

The very next day is Friday, the day of the Snow Ball. It's fairly unusual that the chairgirl of the planning committee has no intention of going to the dance she planned for weeks, but then again, these are unusual times.

I went straight home yesterday. I didn't have to fake a stomachache, because after that, I had a pretty fierce one. And the stupid part is, I was kind of hoping Laurel or Susannah would call me last night. Or Maisie, even, to thank me for freeing her. I wasn't stupid enough to think Riley would call me. And he didn't.

cave

Me hibernating

The only call I got was from Smartin, making sicko-freakboy kissy sounds.

As I'm lying on my bed, not going to the dance, my phone rings. It's Laurel! "Hey, Zoë. My mom says we can't pick you up, so I'll have to meet you at the dance. I'll be the one in—"

I'm so happy she thinks I'm going, I could burst. "Let me guess, blue."

"Nope. Turquoise," she says. She sounds proud.

"Seriously? That's not *quite* blue."

"I know. I'm working my way around the color wheel. Starting with green. Well, starting with not quite green."

"Outrageous," I say. "How's everyone?"

Her voice changes. Gets smaller. "Okay." She pauses. "So meet me at the change-room steps?"

"I'm not going to the dance, Laurel."

There's a long silence, during which I hear a loud, probably blue, hopefully turquoise, slurp. "You have to. You have all the rule sheets. **If you don't come we'll have no rules. It'll be total kiosk.**"

She means it'll be total *chaos,* but I'm too frazzled by the stack of rule sheets on my bedside table to tell her. How could I have forgotten? "Can't your mother pick them up on the way?"

"She can't go that way, I told you. Just stick them in your backpack. See you, there!"

Horrible, stink-o-rotten luck.

Now I have to go to school.
Only I can't go in my current state
of being, which is Garage Girls pj's and
bear-claw slippers. I'm going to have to dress
for the dance to blend in. Walk in fast, keep
my head down, dump off the rules, and get the heck
out of there before anyone notices me. Otherwise I'll never
be able to get back to my slippers and my room, where I
plan to hibernate in my cave forevermore.

*W*ith my backpack slung over one shoulder of my lavender dress, I hurry past the fruit market and around the corner onto Allencroft Boulevard. It's so cold outside I can see my breath. On my way back, when the streetlamps are on, I plan to stand beneath one and see if I can blow smoke rings.

The closer I get to the school, the more I think that maybe *not* going to this dance is exactly the wrong thing to do. That maybe dropping off the rules and running is a really bad idea. **School dances are nerve-taxing group situations and there are bound to be scads of social blunders and desperate requests for advice.** I mean, if I'd thought about it far enough in advance, I could have built myself a secret booth like LameWizard Richard's, and set it up under the basketball hoop. I could have hidden inside and charged a dollar per Unwritten Rule and donated the proceeds to help pay for the pricey blueberry juice and the ginger cookies from the Netherlands.

Besides, it's Susannah's big day, the day she signs for her new commercial that will hopefully mean the end of the dark glasses, and I need to be there to support her and keep sticky fingers away from her hair, which I'm not even sure she owns anymore. It might belong to the hair-care company. Or her agent.

I slip inside the school and follow the blaring music through the halls, toward the gym. And by the time I reach the gym doors, which are closed, probably to keep the boys from running away, I'm feeling a bit better. **Who needs public approval?** I'm pretty sure I still have Laurel, and where there's Laurel, Susannah can't be far behind . . .

Two girls burst out of the gym, laughing, and I grab the door before it swings shut. **What I see inside takes my breath away.**

Balloons. Hundreds and hundreds of balloons in every pastel color imaginable. There are silver balloons floating to the ceiling, star-covered balloons stuck to walls, smiley-face balloons on the snack table, and balloons roaming loose all

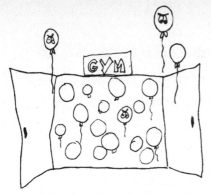

over the dance floor like wild animals, shooting every which way as people kick them and throw them in the air.

I think I'm gonna faint.

My feet step backward. Far away I hear people calling my name, but, I don't know, it might just be the floor balloons tricking me. Dropping my backpack, I spin around and race through the school and out the front doors. People say my name, but I just keep running.

I run past the fruit market and past the bookstore. I run past my apartment building and the dry cleaners and the café with the plastic German shepherd in the window. I run and run until I get there. The gazebo. The secret place.

So secret that it has its own rule. **Unwritten Rule #11 is: Hunters Park gazebo is the most special place on Earth.** No one knows this. Because no one but me knows this rule exists.

I must have been smaller than a mouse when Dad took me here. The gazebo sits on top of a hill, like a pretty little shed that the wind can blow right through, and you can see the whole town from inside it. I still remember it was dark and it started to snow a bit, just light little flakes blowing around, and my dad showed me how, if you look real close, each snowflake really is completely different, just like they say.

He smelled like a wood-burning stove and that smell kept me warm.

But other than him taking that picture of me on the gazebo steps, that's all I remember. **Mom always says I'm not supposed to go to the gazebo hill alone, but my feet don't care.** They take me there as fast as they can.

The gazebo is empty except for a little cat that runs away from all the noise my feet make when I thunder inside. When I drop to the floor, panting, I wish the cat had stayed. My thin coat isn't doing much for me; maybe it could have helped keep him warm. And he could have helped me.

A whistle of wind swirls some dried leaves around the floor and I pull my coat tighter. I think about my bear-claw slippers.

The thing is, **life's a lot of work.** *My* life's a lot of work. But maybe there's a way to lessen the burden without hiring a husband for Mom.

A husband for Grandma, maybe?

Nah. That wouldn't help. It would just make me hate Mondays even more. Double the pills to count.

Suddenly a thought pops into my head. It's a thought I work very hard to make disappear. It has a lot to do with Unwritten Rule #10. Actually it *is* Unwritten Rule #10. And there's a reason I never, ever reveal Unwritten Rule #10 to any of my clients.

Unwritten Rule #10 cancels out rules one to nine. Erases them. Gone.

Unwritten Rule #10 is: Sometimes the Best Way to Be a Friend Is to Just Let People Be Themselves.

I've never liked Unwritten Rule #10.

It interferes with business.

Just then I hear what might be some voices climbing up my hill. I sincerely hope they're not evil-stranger voices, because it's starting to get dark and my feet already hurt from running in fancy shoes.

"Zoë," someone calls. Someone who sounds an awful lot like Susannah. "You up there?"

"In here!" I shout, standing up and peering down the path in the fading light. Like a trail of ants in party clothes, a whole line of kids traipses up the hill.

One by one they file into my gazebo. First Laurel, then Susannah and Maisie, then Avery, Alice, Brianna, Sylvia, Smartin, and, last, Riley. They all stand in a big half circle facing me.

"Zoë," says Susannah. She's still wearing her dark glasses. **"We, the people, have an announcement."**

Behind her I can see big fat snowflakes beginning to swirl and dance in the glow of the lights lining the path. The first real snow of the season.

Maisie steps forward. "I told everyone why you did it. That you were only trying to help me. That what you said wasn't true. Thanks."

Then Smartin laughs and stuffs his hands in his pockets. "I guess deep inside I kinda knew you'd never love *me*." I smile at him because **it's awfully grown up to admit you're too icky for public declarations of love.** It almost makes him more likable.

Laurel takes my hand and says. "You've been awfully good about taking care of the rest of us, for an awfully long time. **And we've decided that it's time we take care of you."**

Susannah, who is still wearing her dark glasses, says, "It's time we give you a clean slate."

"Just like you gave me," Maisie says. She nods toward Susannah and adds, "I just found out the real reason you took me on as a client. Thanks."

Susannah then takes my other hand and they guide me out into the falling snow and onto the path, where snowflakes twinkle and dance in the light of old-fashioned coach lamps, now lit.

"Don't take me back to the gym," I say, pulling backward. "There were too many. It's probably best if we go get doughnuts. Or maybe go straight home."

"Zoë," Riley says, putting his hands on my shoulders. "We're your best friends in the whole world. **Are you going to just stand there, or trust us?**"

"Mm. I don't really know."

"Okay," he says. He looks up to the sky and twists his mouth to one side, making the cutest dimple appear in his cheek. "Here's how much you can trust me. You know how I have to practice every day after school, no exceptions?"

Do I ever! "Yeah."

"I'm not really a sumo wrestler."

"I kinda figured."

He flips up the collar of his jacket. Behind him, both Smartin and Maisie twirl in circles, eyes closed and tongues sticking out to catch snowflakes. **"Wanna know what I really do?"**

I nod so fast I bite my tongue.

Riley leans closer and whispers into my ear, "Ballet."

"Bal—?"

"Shh! I'm trusting you not to tell." He steps back and lifts his eyebrows. Then he pulls a sparkly gold chain from his pocket and fastens it around my neck, where it shimmers in the dark. **"Ready to trust me now? Enough to go to the dance with me?"**

Still touching the necklace, I look at Riley and nod. I step forward and follow him down the hill in the snow. As we pick our way down the path, surrounded by trees and bushes gathering snow on leafless branches, I remember something. "Wait!"

My friends stop moving.

"Susannah! I completely forgot about your hair commercial. Your big meeting was today. Did you sign?"

Susannah sniffs. "I signed."

"What kind of commercial is it going to be?"

"It's really not important," she says, stepping over a fallen branch. **"What's important is I'm a working actress."**

"Does it mean you're finally going to ditch the shades?" I ask.

"No," she says with a sarcastic chuckle. "The shades I'll keep."

"Oh, *please* tell us," Laurel whines. "What kind of commercial is it?"

Susannah stops. She's silent for a moment; her long, lustrous hair is shimmering from a streetlight behind her. She looks around, pushes her sunglasses farther up her nose, and pulls a silky scarf over her head. Then she leans back toward the rest of us and whispers, "Head lice."

$\mathcal{B}$y the time we get back to the dance, my heart is pounding and I'm pretty sure I'm about to faint. But before Riley opens the gym doors, he says, "Everyone remember the rules?"

They nod and Riley says, "Good. **Assume your positions."**

Then they all join hands and form a circle all the way around me, like a cage. And Susannah says to me, "You'll be totally safe."

All of a sudden Neon Pink runs by with an armful of balloons. She's being chased by Bloomer Girl, who's got a balloon between her teeth. Allegra actually looks like she's having fun. So does Pink.

"You mean," I say, swallowing hard, "we're going right inside? With all the balloons?"

They all nod and Maisie pops open a big umbrella. "Nothing will touch you, Zoë. We promise. You're covered on all sides."

Smartin says, "So you can just look around you and be amazed. It's really quite lovely in there."

I'm still reeling from the shock of hearing Smartin use a word like "lovely" when they do the most amazing thing. They move together, cocooning me as we enter the balloon-filled Winter Dance. Not a balloon can touch me; they just float by, like pastel-colored bubbles in a dream. I glance around to see everyone is still holding hands; the umbrella is still sheltering me. My friends have made a human shield all around me.

I'm perfectly safe.

The balloons are actually beautiful. There are lavender balloons floating over us, then we pass a whole archway of pink. It's almost magical. I notice Riley smiling at me and I mouth the words "thank you."

He grins back and goes up on his tippy toes. Like a ballerina boy.

I smile.

From my cocoon, I can see the refreshment table, covered in massive bowls of costly blueberries and big plates of Dutch cookies. And on the stage is what must be the band, with Avery on the keyboard, another kid on the triangle, and Avery's mother setting up the microphone to sing.

Smartin leans close to me. "They were the cheapest. They actually paid us for the gig. It was the only way Brianna could afford the balloons."

We all laugh.

Just then, as I look around in amazement, **I think how much Grandma would love to see me being so brave.** And even though I don't want to ruin this moment with sad thoughts, Grandma's words pop into my head. Don't try to paint spots on a leopard.

Hmm.

Is it possible that Grandma has her very own

set of rules thinly disguised as crazy talk? Because if you think about it, isn't her leopard rule kind of the same as number ten, since the leopard probably has his own spots and maybe doesn't need you, or me, to go around slopping new ones all over him?

And if that's true, then maybe her advice about not being able to polish poodles meant that never in a million years was I going to pluck jaggedy feather stumps off a fleshy chicken. Even her advice about not building a nest on a flagpole made sense! Build your house on solid ground instead of a cliff. That's what she meant. Except if you're a bird. Then you'd better choose a good solid branch so you can see the cats coming.

If Grandma's words are not so strange, doesn't that make Grandma pretty much sane? Maybe it's just that the rest of us are just too thick to get what she's been saying all this time!

I burst through my friends' arms and start to run through the balloons. Balloons crash up and hit me in the stomach, face, arms. Susannah and Riley call to me, but I don't have time to explain. I have to get home before Mom signs the Shady Gardens papers. I have to tell her I just figured out what Grandma's been saying!

o o o

I don't stop for anything, not for my coat and certainly not for the old man begging for quarters out front of the A&P. I race all the way home and don't even stop for the elevator. Mom could be up there right now, with Jason, signing Grandma away. I run up the eight flights of stairs and arrive, huffing and puffing, at the eighth-floor landing. But when I open the heavy door into the hallway, I see it's kind of smoky and firemen walk in and out of somebody's apartment.

The closer I get, the more I cough and the more I realize the smoke and firemen are coming from my apartment! I rush inside to find Mom at the kitchen table talking to someone on the phone. When she sees me, she looks relieved. "Never mind, Mr. Lindsay," she says into the phone. "She's just walked in."

"What?" I shout. "What happened? Where's Grandma?"

Mom pulls me onto her lap and strokes my hair. "Grandma's fine. They've taken her to Hillside General just to make sure. But now that you're here, we'll go check on her."

"But what happened?" I look around to see a mess on the stove.

Mom sighs. "Grandma left a newspaper on the stovetop

and it caught fire. When the firefighters arrived, she was asleep in her room. Thankfully, nothing happened but a whole lot of smoke." She pauses and takes me by the shoulders, looking into my eyes. **"But it could have been much worse."**

I nod.

"You can see now, honey, that the best place for Grandma is a place where she'll be properly supervised. Where she can't be a danger to herself or anyone else. **Do you understand now, Zoë?"**

I bury my head in Mom's shoulder and breathe in her smell. My eyes slide closed because I can't keep them open anymore. "Yes," I whisper.

Sometimes Happy Comes in Extra Chunky

Sunlight is pouring through Grandma's window on Sunday morning. It's so bright it almost makes her beige flowery wallpaper look like a pretty yellow. I think the extra brightness has something to do with the sunny rays bouncing off the snow that fell last night. It covered the Shady Gardens with sparkle.

After they released Grandma from the hospital yesterday morning, we took her straight to the nursing home, where they'll watch her better than me or Mom ever could. The room overlooking the butterfly garden had already been "snapped up," as Mom said, so **Gram got this other room way closer to the snack room.** Which is good. And it's closer to the nurses' station, where Frisbee, the old collie, sleeps. Also good.

Another thing that got snapped up is Get-me-this-Get-me-that Jason. I guess he did such a good job of locking up old people here at Shady Gardens, he got hired by some gigantic retirement home in Florida, where he can eat some other girl's butterscotch squares. He moves away next month.

Grandma's sitting in her brown flowery chair watching *Jeopardy!* and asking why Alex Trebek isn't wearing his pitcher's uniform. Mom and me, who are on the sofa, try to explain that baseball won't be on until the spring. **Grandma's room isn't nearly as dumpy-looking as the rooms in the pictures,** and I'm pretty sure they haven't made her get her picture taken to prove how much she loves it there.

Grandma also has a brand-new boyfriend, Rex. He lives two flowery bedrooms away and they've already been caught sharing a cigar in the game room. Mom was mad that Grandma was breaking Shady Gardens' rules after less than twenty-four hours, but I was just glad Grandma was feeling good enough to have fun. She might even see that happy comes in extra-big chunks—chunks way bigger than sixty seconds.

"Mom," I say, turning to face my mother, "will Grandma ever be back?"

She pats my hand. "Absolutely. She'll come and go. Some

days will be better than others. But you'll know it when she's here with you."

Then Grandma looks straight at me and says, **"Why don't you have some candy, little girl?"**

I stand up. "Okay. Thanks, Grandma." I help myself to a couple of red cinnamon hearts and pour them into my mouth, where they burn my tongue with their spiciness.

As I pass her chair, Grandma touches my shoulder and stops me. "You're welcome, Zoë."

With a happy glance at my mom, I climb onto Grandma's lap and give her the biggest hug I can manage without thumping her with my cast. "I love you, Gram," I whisper. But her eyes have gone blank. She's gone again.

Just then a tall nurse comes in with Grandma's lunch. She smiles at us and sets the tray on the bedside table. "Lunchtime, Mrs. Costello."

It looks like a turkey sandwich with a wilted salad and some green Jell-O. Which Grandma should like. I take the cover off the coffee cup and am happy to find it isn't coffee, but hot cocoa. Only some of the chocolate powder isn't dissolved and it smells like the milk's been scalded.

Hmm. I don't want my grandma drinking second-rate cocoa.

There really should be somebody in the kitchen watching over the food preparation. At least important things like cocoa preparation. Someone who knows that you have to add the cocoa slowly and keep stirring it until all the little chunks dissolve.

What this place needs are a few rules.

I look up at the nurse, whose tag says HILARY BANKS. "Excuse me," I say. "Hilary, is it? I'm something of an expert when it comes to chocolate. Did you make the cocoa yourself?"

She looks surprised, but she nods.

"I see." I take her big hand in mine and guide her out the door. "If you've got a moment, I'd like to take you back to the kitchen and share a few Unwritten Rules I have when it comes to making cocoa."

"Rules?" she asks. "Are they from a cookbook?"

"No. They're *unwritten.*"

"Ah," she says as we pass Frisbee in his dog bed. "That would make them invisible."

I sigh. I'll wait until after I get my cocoa to tell her I prefer my rules unwritten.

On Monday morning, things are back to normal at school. Not only has **Brianna apologized for photocopying the love letter** and sprinkling it around the school to get back at Maisie for spilling the Brinderella beans, she's also decided that 14 million balloons aren't the best idea for a Snow Ball, since, in order to get rid of them, you have to pop every single one that survived the dance. **She spent the whole weekend in the gym with her mother's knitting needles.**

Sylvia walks by me on the way to her locker before first period. She smiles like she's got some big secret. "Hi, Zoë. Seen Riley yet?"

"No. Why?"

"No reason." And she hurries to homeroom.

Then Maisie and Laurel pass by. "Hey, Zoë. Have a nice weekend?" They say it together, like they planned it.

"Yes," I say. "And why didn't you guys take my phone calls? I was dying to know what happened at the dance after I left."

They giggle. "You'll see," says Laurel. And they walk off like a pair of figure skaters.

Just as I'm about to swing into homeroom, Riley pops his head out of a janitor's closet. "*Psst!* Zoë, in here."

I check my watch. "But it's almost eight forty-five. I don't want to be late."

"Drop your rules for once and get in here."
He grabs my arm above the cast and pulls me into the tiny room, which is filled with rags and hoses and bottles of cleaner and . . . Avery?

"Congratulations, Zoë," Avery says, sitting on an upside-down bucket with his keyboard on his lap.

"What's going on?" I ask, dropping my books onto a shelf full of sponges. "Congratulations for what?"

Riley just smiles and pulls out a gold crown. He lifts it high in the air and lowers it onto his head.

"You?" I squeak with joy. "You were crowned Snow Ball King? Did you get to dance with Susannah?"

He shakes his head and pulls another crown from the shelf behind him. It's all gold and sparkly plastic with fake rubies and diamonds glued all over the front. It's beautiful. He says, "I haven't had my royal dance yet." Then he pushes my hair away from my eyes and sets the crown on my head. "My Snow Ball Queen had to leave early."

"You mean . . . me? They elected me?"

Grinning, he nods. "*We* elected you." He puts one arm around my waist and the other one around my cast. Avery starts playing something really awful on his keyboard. Really awful and really romantic. He keeps hitting the wrong keys and stopping to whisper-curse, and at one point he knocks over a few mops, but I don't care.

I'm dancing with my king.

*A*s we sit with our instruments on our laps, waiting for our music teacher, my head—or maybe it's my heart—is still buzzing from my royal dance. There are three things I can't get out of my mind (and I never, ever want to!):

1. the smell of bleach,
2. Avery's pinching his pinky finger in the keys, and
3. the feeling of Riley's arms wrapped around me as we swayed back and forth.

Five minutes after Mrs. Day should have started waving her baton, a youngish older guy with shaggy brown hair and faded jeans walks up to her music stand and smiles.

"Good morning class. I'm Jet Rankin. Your regular teacher, Mrs. Day, had to leave the country indefinitely on an urgent family matter. So it looks like I'm going to be your music teacher until she returns." He blushes and wavy hair falls over one eye. "Put down your instruments for a bit. I want you all to introduce yourselves. Tell me who you are and what you're all about."

He doesn't have to ask me twice! I drop my trumpet with a clatter.

From the saxophone section, Susannah puts up her hand. **"Can we start with you? Who *you* are and what *you're* all about?"**

He laughs and runs a hand through his hair. His teeth are nice and white. "Sure, but I'm a pretty dull guy. I've been teaching for thirteen years, I love kids, and I'm what my mother calls 'an organizer.' So if you find me polishing and putting away your instruments for you, don't be alarmed."

Am I dreaming?

"It might sound strange, but nothing gives me more pleasure than doing things for other people."

Just as I'm wondering if his wife knows how lucky she is, Laurel blurts out, "Like your wife?" You gotta love Laurel.

He leans forward and laughs again. Then he rubs his stubbly chin and sighs. "No such luck. I'm still single."

Single? I sit up a little taller. Then I remember Unwritten Rule #12, the newest of all the rules. I can't remember it exactly, but it had something to do with leaving my mother's love life alone. Forever.

A smile spreads across my face because a new rule just popped into my head. **Unwritten Rule #13. Which is, Rules Were Made to Be Smashed Beyond Recognition.**

Jet says, "Before I turn the floor over to you guys, does anyone have any questions? Suggestions for the class?"

All around the room, hands shoot up. Including mine.

Jet points at me. "The girl in the trumpet section. Question or suggestion?"

"Question." I say, thinking Hunters Park gazebo would be the perfect place for a spring wedding. **"When's Parents' Night?"**